**Walt Disney Productions...**

***Adapted by MEL CEBULASH from the Walt Disney motion picture***

Screenplay by Bill Walsh and Don DaGradi
Based on a story by Gordon Buford

SCHOLASTIC BOOK SERVICES
NEW YORK • TORONTO • LONDON • AUCKLAND • SYDNEY • TOKYO

 Published by Scholastic Book Services, a division of Scholastic Magazines, Inc. by arrangement with Walt Disney Productions.

**12th printing . . . . . . . . . . . . . . . . . . . . . . . December 1973**

Printed in the U.S.A.

*CAST*

| | |
|---|---|
| DEAN JONES | JIM |
| MICHELE LEE | CAROLE |
| DAVID TOMLINSON | THORNDYKE |
| BUDDY HACKETT | TENNESSEE |
| JOE FLYNN | HAVERSHAW |
| BENSON FONG | MR. WU |
| JOE E. ROSS | DETECTIVE |
| BARRY KELLEY | POLICE SGT. |
| IRIS ADRIAN | CARHOP |

*And*

HERBIE

*Of the many millions of small cars that rolled off the assembly lines, it happened that one was different from all the others.*

# I

JIM DOUGLAS stomped hard on the gas pedal. The wreck that he was driving picked up a little speed, and he wheeled it into the side of a yellow car. The yellow car rolled over and then disappeared into one of the clouds of dust sprinkled around the race track.

It was Destruction Derby. The rules were simple. While the people in the stands cheered and groaned, the old cars on the track tried to wreck each other. Then when all the cars, except one, were knocked out of action, the driver of that remaining car won the prize money.

Jim shifted into reverse and let his clutch out slowly. He searched the track for cars still running. Hearing the loud cheers coming from the stands, he wondered if he already had won the prize money.

Just then Jim spotted the only other car running on the track. It was coming right at him, and there was no time to get out of its way. The other car plowed into Jim's wreck, snapping Jim's face into his steering wheel and putting his car out of action.

A young man, several years younger than Jim, climbed out of the winning car seconds later and waved to the people in the stands. At the same time, Jim staggered away from his wreck and headed for the dressing rooms. Blood trickled from a long cut on the side of his face.

After a hot shower, Jim felt much better. He stood before a mirror, examining the damage done to his face. It was a cut, and it would heal. It wasn't the first cut he had gotten sitting behind the wheel of a car.

"Jim Douglas still here?" Mr. Bice, the promoter of the Derby, called from the entrance to the dressing rooms.

"Right here," Jim said. "What can I do for you?"

"Get dressed, and I'll drive you into the city," Bice said. "I'll be out in the parking lot waiting for you."

Later, Jim looked at the man driving him home and said, "Mr. Bice, I'd like another chance at that prize money. How about next Sunday?"

"No, Jim," the Derby promoter said, "not next Sunday or any other Sunday."

"Wait a minute!" Jim said.

"You wait a minute!" Bice said, glancing over at Jim. "All my drivers are eighteen, maybe nineteen years old. You're getting too old for these kid events. You used to be a big track driver. Don't you have any pride?"

Jim shrugged his shoulders. "I ran out of pride when I ran out of cars."

"You're a Jonah—a bad luck guy," Bice said. "You took some good cars out and sprayed them all over the track. Now people don't trust you with their expensive machinery. Maybe they have a point."

"Maybe they do," Jim said.

"So quit, kid," Bice suggested. "I got a brother-in-law

who owns a used car lot. He can always use a mechanic."

Speaking softly, Jim said, "Thanks, but I'm not a mechanic."

"Well, you ought to get a job doing something else," Bice said. "Maybe you had something once, but you've come to the end of the line now."

For the rest of the ride, Jim kept silent. Bice was wrong. Jim still could win against the best drivers in the business. He felt sure of that. All he needed was a break — a chance to get started again.

When they reached the old firehouse that Jim and his friend, Tennessee Steinmetz, had turned into a combination apartment and garage, Jim climbed out of the car and thanked Bice for the lift.

"Need any money?" Bice asked.

"No," Jim said. "I'm all right."

Instead of going into the firehouse, Jim walked around to the courtyard. There he found Tennessee, welding another piece of metal onto a growing pile of junk. Tennessee, who looked and talked like Buddy Hackett, regarded his sculptured pile of parts from wrecked autos as a work of art.

Hearing Jim's footsteps, Tennessee lifted his welder's mask and turned to face his roommate. "How did it go, Jim?"

But before Jim could answer, Tennessee noticed the cut on his face. "You got hurt again," he said.

"Forget it," Jim said, turning toward the firehouse. "Come on. I'm hungry."

Inside the firehouse, Jim started searching the cupboards and refrigerator for food. He didn't notice that Tennessee's car, an Edsel, was missing.

"Maybe racing ain't your thing," Tennessee said. "A

top mechanic certainly gets plenty of bread laid on him."

Hearing that suggestion again angered Jim. "What's the matter with everybody?" he said. "I'm not a mechanic! Can't you understand that?"

"I know how you feel, Jim," Tennessee said softly. "I used to think I was happy painting flower seeds, but this tiny voice way down inside me kept saying, 'Pal, you ain't happy!' "

"Wait a minute!" Jim said, holding up a bag of dried leaves from the health food store. "Why is it there's never anything around here but this parrot food? We don't even *have* a parrot!"

"That chopped kelp is good for you, Jim," Tennessee said, determined to get on with his story. "Anyway, the small voice kept talking. It said, 'You are nowhere, pal. You got to make a new scene. Change your bag.' That's when I split. I go to live out in Tibet, rapping with them monks and swamis on a mountain top. Finally, I plug in with the contemplation and find my real self."

"Look, I know who I am, and I know what I want," Jim said. "Right now I plan to pick up a few bucks at the dirt track races near Bakersfield this week. You mind if I borrow the beast to get there?"

Tennessee didn't answer, and Jim noticed that the Edsel was missing. Quickly, he moved out into the courtyard again. His eyes ran up Tennessee's sculptured monster until they reached what remained of the front of the Edsel.

"All of a sudden, it come over me," Tennessee explained. "It was the only thing to do. The beast is happier up there. I know it."

Jim staggered back into the house.

He couldn't blame Tennessee for doing his thing, but he knew that finding a car — any kind of car — for the money he had to spend wasn't going to be easy.

Early the next day, Jim visited a used car lot, but the salesman didn't have one car for the price that Jim mentioned. So Jim wandered on down the street until he came to a very fancy foreign car agency named "Peter Thorndyke, Limited." Anxious to see some of the new high-priced foreign beauties, he stopped, but instead of focusing on cars, his eyes were attracted to two pretty legs below a sign that read, "May We Direct Your Attention to These."

Jim grinned, moving closer to the showroom window and glancing around the edge of the sign. He and the girl with the pretty legs came face to face. Surprised by him, she dropped the lower half of the sign, and Jim, forgetting the plate glass window that separated them, reached down for the sign and banged his head. When he looked up, he saw the girl signaling him to come inside.

"I'm really very sorry," the girl told Jim, as she applied some ointment to his bruised head.

"It was my fault," Jim said. "I guess I surprised you."

Then the girl introduced herself, and Jim did the same, but his eyes and thoughts drifted to a big, sleek yellow Apollo spinning slowly on a display turntable. He drifted over to the turntable and stared at the shiny foreign car, and the girl rushed to his side.

"I'll see to the gentleman," Mr. Peter Thorndyke, the owner of the agency, told the girl. "May I be of service, sir?"

Jim just stood there, looking dreamily at the Apollo and mumbling about its finer points. A look of joy spread over Thorndyke's face, and he got a bottle of wine and two glasses. Then he asked Jim, "May I offer you sherry?"

MAY WE
DIRECT YOUR
ATTENTION
TO THESE

"Go right ahead," Jim said, still staring at the Apollo.

Pouring the wine, Thorndyke said, "I'm sure the matter of price does not concern a gentleman like yourself?"

"Well, I wouldn't try to bargain, if that's what you mean."

Thorndyke smiled. "What price range did you have in mind?"

"I'd say about seventy-five dollars," Jim answered. "But I suppose I could go to eighty, if I really liked the car."

Thorndyke's smile disappeared. He quickly poured the sherry back into the bottle. Then he said, "I will bid you good day, sir."

Jim smiled, as Thorndyke marched off. Then a small car rolled into the showroom and gently touched Jim. He looked for the driver, but there was no one behind the wheel, so he opened the little car's door and pulled up the handbrake. When he finished, Thorndyke was back, calling angrily for a Mr. Havershaw. A short man came running over, followed by the girl who had invited Jim into the showroom.

"Mr. Havershaw," Thorndyke screamed, "what is this thing doing in my showroom?"

Havershaw turned to the girl and said, "Miss Bennett may know something about it, sir."

"I do," the girl said calmly. "When Mrs. Hergit purchased her Bentley, she also requested us to buy a small used car for her maid."

"Then why isn't Mrs. Hergit's maid in her car?" Thorndyke said.

"The car was returned this morning," Miss Bennett explained. "The maid was having some difficulty with it."

"Well, get it out of here!" Thorndyke said, kicking the

side of the little car as hard as he possibly could.

That kick angered Jim. "Why don't you let the little car alone?" he said.

"Are you telling me what to do in my showroom?" Thorndyke replied.

"I guess I'm out of line," Jim admitted. "But I just get bugged when I see some idiot abusing a decent piece of machinery."

"How very fascinating," Thorndyke said, turning away from Jim. "Havershaw, you get this thing out of my showroom, and if I ever see this little car again, someone is going to find himself in a great deal of trouble."

Jim headed for the exit, while Havershaw and another salesman tried to push the little car out of the showroom. The little car locked its wheels and seemed to be fighting against the two salesmen. Then Jim turned. He was facing the little car, but his eyes and mind were on the Apollo. Finally, he went outside and got on the first cable car that came along.

Seconds later, the little car came racing out of an alley alongside the showroom and followed the cable car. Again, the little car had no one behind its wheel!

A steady buzzing of the doorbell ended Jim's sleep early the next morning. He walked over to the upstairs bedroom window and looked down. He saw a police car. Then he called to the man ringing his bell, "What do you want?"

"What does he want?" Tennessee said, moving alongside Jim.

"I don't know," Jim said.

After showing his police identification, the man said, "Have you ever seen that car before?"

OFP 857

978

Jim's eyes followed the man's finger as it swung toward the courtyard — and the little car!

"How do you like that?" Jim said. "That looks like a car I saw yesterday at an agency."

"Say no more," the man said. "Say nothing that would take away your constitutional rights. Second, we suggest you call a good lawyer the moment you get downtown. Third, dress nice and warm, because there's a slight breeze coming down from the north. Now shall we go?"

"Go where?" Jim said, puzzled by the sight of the little car and the detective's suggestions.

"Go to the station to be booked on suspicion of grand theft!" the detective explained. "Or to put it another way, we are beginning to entertain the idea that you neglected to tell the owner of this car that you were taking it home."

"Now wait a minute!" Jim said. "There's something crazy going on here. How did that car get here?"

"I share your curiosity, sir," the detective replied. "Shall we go? And let me thank you in advance for your splendid cooperation."

While Jim dressed, he told Tennessee everything that had happened at Thorndyke's car agency. Then he said, "How do you suppose that little car got here?"

Tennessee smiled. "Maybe it followed you, Jim."

Jim did not smile back. Minutes later, he was in the police car on the way to the station house.

## 11

THE DETECTIVE telephoned Thorndyke's agency from the police station. Thorndyke hadn't arrived there yet, so the detective spoke to Miss Bennett, telling her where the car had been found and that the agency would have to send someone to pick it up. Then he told her that the suspect's name was Jim Douglas. The conversation continued for several more minutes, but the detective said very little, and Jim wondered if Carole Bennett remembered him.

"Well, Douglas," the detective said, setting the phone back in place, "Miss Bennett seems to think that you have an honest face and that you deserve a chance to speak to Mr. Thorndyke, before we take your fingerprints and picture and other things like that. So I will drive you over to Mr. Thorndyke's agency, and if you are lucky, I won't have to drive you back here."

At the agency, Thorndyke indicated that he doubted Jim's story about the mysterious appearance of the little car in his courtyard, and Jim indicated that he was beginning to think that Thorndyke had placed the car in Jim's courtyard. The two of them argued, while Miss Bennett worked out an arrangement for Jim to be free of the charges and buy the little car with monthly payments.

Finally, Thorndyke said, "All right, Miss Bennett, see that Mr. Douglas signs the necessary papers. Then see that he and his car get out of here before I lose my temper!"

The detective left, and Thorndyke walked over to the little car. He was glad to be rid of it — glad that Douglas was buying it. It certainly didn't belong to *his* agency. Then he looked down and saw oil shooting from a valve under the little car onto his feet.

Jim drove out of the agency in his little car a short time later. He cruised around the city for a few miles, and then he decided to test the little car at higher speeds on the Bay Shore Freeway.

Jim drove down the first on-ramp he could find and huge trailer trucks whizzed by the little car's front end. Suddenly the little car let out a strange sound — almost like the scream of a frightened woman. After that, the little car's brake pedal slammed down — by itself!

Noticing the pedal, Jim reached down and tried to pull it out. From then on, the little car took charge. It shifted itself into reverse, let out its brake pedal, and backed wildly down the ramp, throwing Jim to the floor.

Minutes later, the little car, with Jim trying to regain control of its wheel, came racing into the alley behind Thorndyke's agency. The sound of the little car's skid stopped Miss Bennett who was just about to climb into Thorndyke's new Rolls Royce. She and Thorndyke turned and saw the little car was running itself and its target seemed to be Thorndyke.

The frightened agency owner managed to jump out of

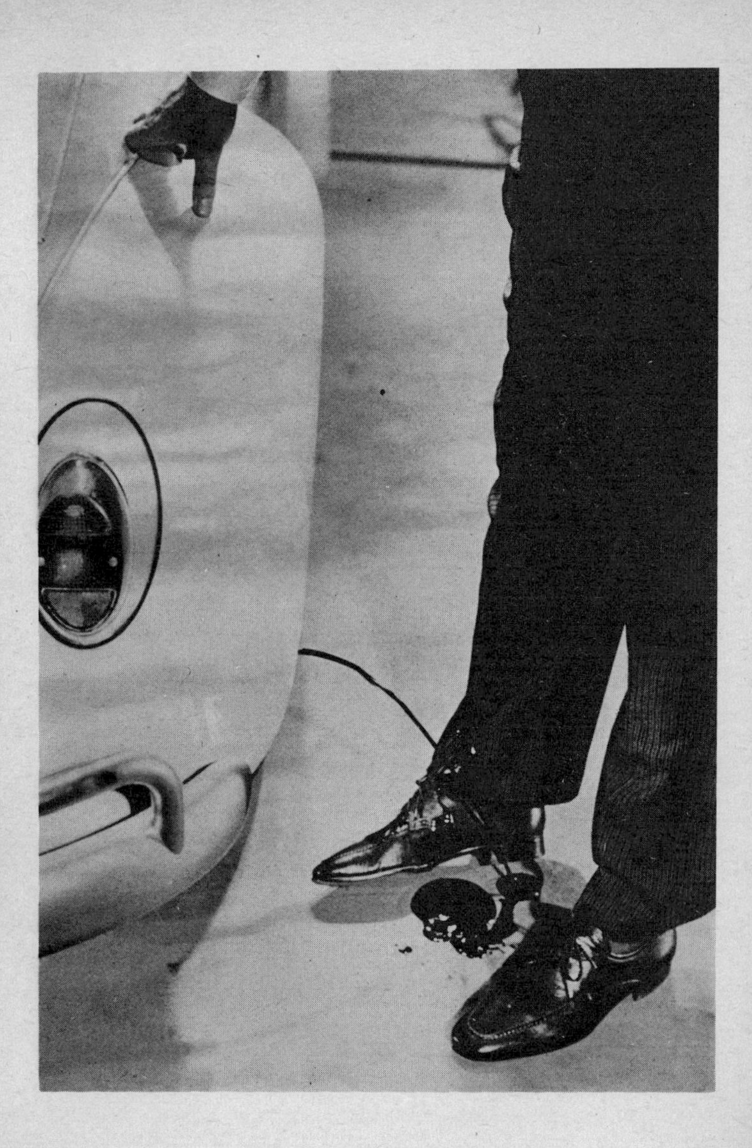

the way, and the little car skidded into the trunk of his Rolls Royce and bounced off it.

"Have you gone mad?" Thorndyke screamed, as Jim climbed out of the little car.

Jim pointed to the little car and said, "Look, I brought the thing back. I don't know how you get that little thing to do its tricks, but I'll just take my money back, and you two can get your laughs some other way."

"If there is anything wrong with this car, will you please tell me what it is?" Miss Bennett asked.

Jim grinned and said, "Well, there's nothing really wrong. When I want to go one way, the car goes another way. That's about all."

"Our guarantee doesn't cover that," Thorndyke said.

"Wait! I sold this gentleman the car, so I feel responsible for it," Miss Bennett said, turning to Jim. "Do you mind if I try it?"

Jim climbed into the passenger seat, while Miss Bennett slipped in behind the wheel. He hoped the little car would do its tricks without killing the both of them.

"Our dinner engagement!" Thorndyke called to Miss Bennett.

She smiled and started the car. "I won't be a minute."

To Jim's surprise, the little car did whatever the pretty girl driving it wanted. "Miss Bennett," he said, "I don't know what to say."

"Call me Carole," she said, "and I'll call you Jim. Now have you had much experience with cars?"

"Look, Carole," Jim said angrily, "car racing is my business. I'm a driver."

Carole thought for a moment and then said, "Oh, *that* Jim Douglas!"

"What do you mean by *that?*"

"Two years ago you hung a beautiful Buick Special on the back fence at Laguna Seca," she said. "At Willow Springs this year, you sprayed a Lotus all over the infield."

"How'd you know all that?" Jim asked.

"I have trouble with names and faces, but I never forget a good car," Carole said. "So suppose you give this little car a fair chance."

At the next stop light, Carole motioned for Jim to drive, and slid into the passenger's seat, while he walked around to the driver's side of the car. As he got into the seat, a young boy and his girl drove up. Grinning at Jim's little car, the boy raced his own engine and yelled to Jim, "Want to give that little bug a workout, Dad? I'll go easy on you!"

Jim wasn't in any mood for dragging, but when the light changed to go, the boy roared away from the corner, and his jalopy coughed exhaust into the little car's face.

The little car reared up onto its back wheels like a wild stallion, throwing Jim and Carole backward in their seats. Then it shot forward with an amazing burst of speed, and its two surprised passengers hung on, as the little car zoomed by the boy and girl in the jalopy. Then it slid to a squealing halt at the next stop sign and shifted down to a low gear.

Turning to Carole, Jim said, "Did you see this thing take off?"

"Was that one of your tricks?" Carole said.

"Believe me," Jim said, "I had nothing to do with it."

Carole opened the door and then said, "I guess the car pleases you now, so I'll just hop out and call a cab."

Without any warning, the door slammed shut, and the little car raced ahead, throwing Carole against Jim.

Angrily, she said, "Will you please stop the car?"

Jim looked down. His foot was pushing against the brake pedal, but it wasn't responding. Then he jiggled the ignition key, but it refused to turn. "It's starting to act up again," he said, bewildered by what was happening.

Returning to the alley behind Thorndyke's, the little car roared at the agency owner again. Thorndyke, who was standing in front of his car waiting for Carole, couldn't believe his eyes. But as the little car came closer and Jim could be seen trying to get it under control, Thorndyke dove behind his car's fender. The little car thundered by and out into the street again.

Jim and Carole's ride continued into the night, and though Carole wanted out, it was clear that Jim had no control over the little car.

Finally, Jim said, "I'm sorry about your engagement. I didn't want you to miss your dinner."

Jim's words sparked the little car. It turned sharply and pulled into a drive-in restaurant. The place seemed filled, but the little car slid into an open spot and honked its horn.

A carhop, grinding the sugar out of a stick of gum, strutted over to the little car and slapped two menus onto its windshield.

Carole tried her door, but it wouldn't open. Then Jim reached over to help. "I can do it myself," she said, pushing his hand away.

Jim watched her struggle unsuccessfully with the door, until the carhop returned. "All right, what'll it be?" she said.

"We've got a little problem," Jim said. "Would you help the young lady get her car door open?"

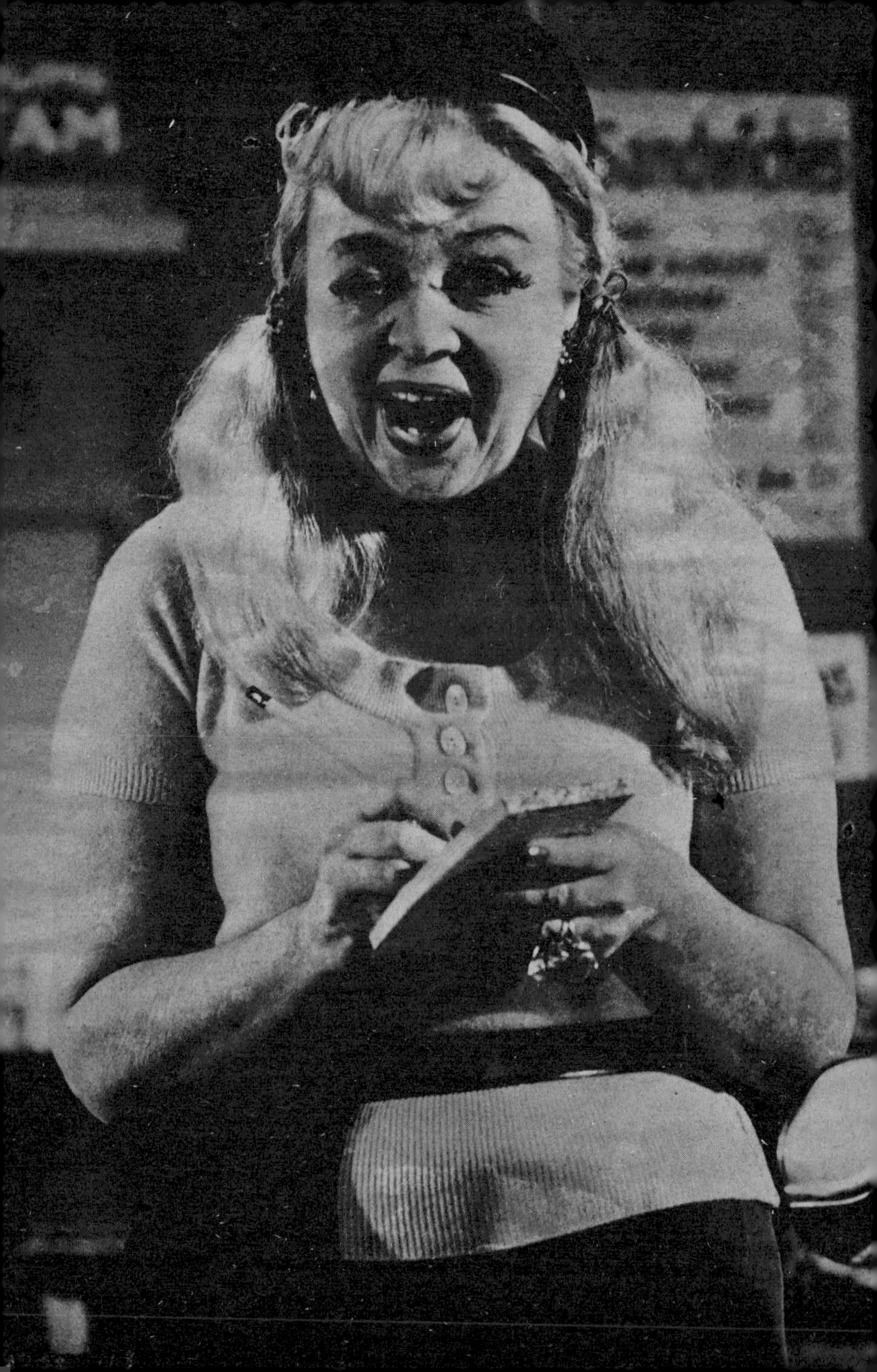

Looking annoyed, the carhop said, "I'm busy, and besides that, do I look like a mechanic? All I do here is sell food — and *that* ain't too good. Now what do you want?"

Carole then called for help, and Jim ordered two hamburgers and a coffee. The carhop went for the order, while Carole continued to call for help and bang on the door. Finally, she got the attention of two hippies seated in an old truck in the spot next to her.

"I'm a prisoner!" she called. "I can't get out!"

The hippies looked at her knowingly. Then one of them said, "We all prisoners, chickie baby. We all of us locked in."

Carole fell back into her seat, but she wasn't ready to admit defeat. This time, she tried to climb over Jim and out his window.

"Hey!" the carhop said, standing by Jim's window with the food tray in her hand. "This ain't the classiest joint in town, but we got to draw the line somewhere! So how about climbing back in your seat!"

"Please help me!" Carole begged.

"All right, sister," the carhop said. "Go up to Seabreeze Point. The fuzz don't bother you much up there."

After Jim and Carole finished eating, the little car pulled away from the drive-in, but Jim seemed to get control over it on the road a few minutes later.

"You know, if I were driving," Carole said, "I'm quite sure none of these things would have happened."

Suddenly, the little car stopped, and Jim guessed that it was trying to tell him to let Carole drive. He got out and walked around the car; Carole slid into the driver's seat.

The car started easily. "Now you'll see what's what!" Carole said proudly.

Minutes later, the little car roared up the road to Seabreeze Point, while Carole frantically tried to turn its wheel. It slid into a spot near the other parked cars and stopped. Carole quickly twisted the ignition key, but the little car refused to start.

Looking out at the moonlit ocean and moving toward Carole, Jim said, "I usually like to know a girl a little longer before . . ."

"Just a minute!" Carole said, holding him away. "You don't dare to think I drove here on purpose?"

"Well," Jim said smiling, "you did bring me here."

Then Carole pushed him and said, "I did not! It's this nasty minded little car!"

Again, he moved toward her, and again, she pushed him away. "You bring this car in tomorrow," she said, "and we'll find another one for you."

"I don't want another one," Jim said, opening his door. "I'm beginning to like this car, but before you panic, I'll see if there's someplace I can phone for a cab."

Jim walked off, and when he was out of sight, Carole tried the ignition key again. To her surprise, the little car started right up. She quickly slid into the driver's seat, shifted the car into low gear, and started down the hill. Then she saw Jim. He had heard the little car's engine and was waiting for Carole, but she just smiled, waved and raced by him.

The little car halted, throwing Carole forward over the wheel. It shifted itself into reverse and backed up to Jim, swinging its passenger side door open. Jim got in, and Carole got out and started down the hill as fast as she could walk. Jim got out of the car went after her, and seconds later, the little car went after both of them.

A policeman parked near the bottom of the hill saw Carole first. Then he saw Jim and the little car moving slowly behind him. The policeman walked over to Carole and reached her just as Jim caught up with her.

"This man bothering you?" the policeman said.

Carole glanced at Jim and realized that she didn't want to get him into trouble. "Well, I wouldn't call it bothering," she said.

"Everything's all right, officer," Jim added. "We're together."

The policeman's attention turned to the little car which had stopped a few feet away. "Is that your car?" he said.

"Yes," Jim said, climbing into the passenger seat, while Carole got into the driver's side.

"You know, you're lucky that I'm not going to write you up," the policeman said. "The next time you decide to walk around a park make sure you pull up the handbrake on your car."

"We certainly will," Carole said, pulling past the policeman and driving for the park exit.

The policeman shook his head and turned back to his own car. It was gone! Then he saw it. The police car had rolled into a nearby pond and was stuck in water up to its windows. He watched, not believing his eyes, as two ducks swam out of his open front window.

In the meantime, the little car seemed under control again, and Carole drove it up to her front door. "This is where I live," she said, stepping out of the car. "Though for a while, I thought I'd never see my door again."

"I'm really sorry," Jim said.

"Well, I guess it wasn't your fault," she said. "I'm still not sure what happened. It's all very strange. Anyhow, goodnight, Jim."

"Goodnight," Jim said, watching her go into her home and hoping that he would see her again.

Then he shifted the little car into low and started off for home. It moved smoothly through the streets and did everything that Jim wanted it to do. Why had the little car performed so strangely most of the day? Jim didn't know, but he felt confident that everything the little car had done could be explained.

"When we get home," he told the little car, "I'm going to find out what makes you tick."

## III

It was late when Jim reached home, but he wanted to examine the little car before going to sleep. He pulled it into the firehouse and opened its hood. Minutes later, Tennessee came in from the courtyard wearing his welder's mask.

"I thought you'd be sleeping by now," Jim said.

"Well, I found a Packard hubcap this evening," Tennessee said, "and the little voice deep inside me kept saying, 'Weld it on!' Meanwhile, does the return of this pretty little car mean that our gentle friend from the police department will be visiting again tomorrow morning?"

Jim explained everything, including the strange actions of the little car, while he poked around its engine trying to find answers to his own questions.

"Well, I knew it would happen," Tennessee said sadly. "Now it's already starting to happen."

"What's starting to happen?"

"Us human beings had a chance to make something out of this world," Tennessee said. "We blew it, though. Now

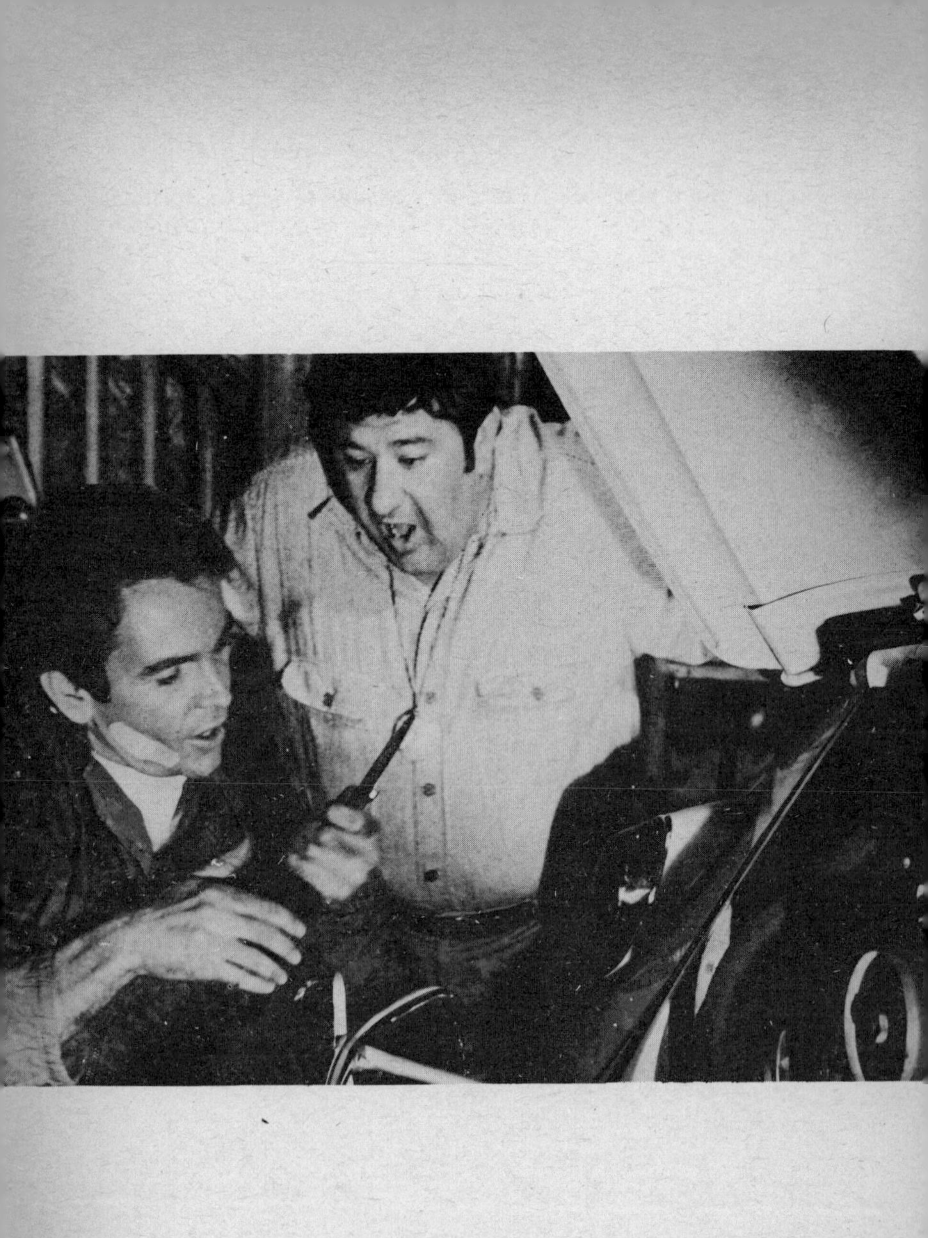

some other kind of civilization is going to take a turn."

Jim got a wrench and went back to work on the little car's engine.

"I'm sitting on this mountain with all the swamis, monks, and gurus around me," Tennessee continued. "I'm looking out at my stomach, and I got some contemplation going. I see things like they are. I see that all this was coming."

"What was coming?"

"The machines," Tennessee said very seriously. "We stuff them full of information and teach them to be smarter than we are. A car is a good example. We give more love and time and money for it than our wives and kids get all year. Pretty soon the machine starts to get an idea that it is somebody."

Reaching for another wrench, Jim said, "I think you were on that mountain top too long."

"Oh, I'm not saying a mechanical thing can't be a friend. When I was broke one summer, there was this giant claw machine out at the amusement park. The claw used to drop cameras and watches down the hole to me. I could sell them and buy lunch. That claw was a real friend.

"On the other hand, that traffic light down at the corner hates my guts. I never did anything to it, but still it gives me the stop sign every time, and it makes me wait six seconds longer than anyone else. I timed it. Other people have things like that happen to them all the time."

Jim faced his friend. "Tennessee, that traffic light is just a lot of nuts and bolts just like this car. Everything finally explains itself one way or another."

"I don't think you got the picture," Tennessee said sadly.

"I got it," Jim said. "What this car did tonight was caused by some kind of mechanical problems. I just haven't found them yet, but the real picture is that this little bug can turn on the speed. You know how it is. They make a thousand cars exactly the same way, but one or two turn out to be something special. Now I could be kidding myself, but I think I can make something out of this motorized beetle."

After closing the little car's hood, Jim went upstairs to the bedroom, while Tennessee got a blanket and gently folded it over the little car's rear deck. "I'm your friend," he whispered, patting the little car's roof. "If you need anything during the night call me."

Then Tennessee hurried upstairs. There Jim explained that he was going to take the little car out for a test run in the morning. Tennessee said that he would go along for the ride. Minutes later, Jim was fast asleep, dreaming about races he would win with the speediest little beetle in the world, and Tennessee was also fast asleep, snoring.

On the freeway the next morning, Jim said, "What did I tell you? This little bug runs like an electric clock."

"Yeah," Tennessee agreed. "Herbie's all right."

"Who's Herbie?" Jim said.

"The little car. I named it after my Uncle Herb who used to be a fighter. After a few fights, his nose got to look like this little car. Do you mind?"

Jim smiled. "No, I'm not sure how you figured out that this little beetle is a male, but Herbie's fine with me."

The little car's performance pleased Jim, and later that day he entered himself and Herbie into a race being held at the end of the week at Jackrabbit Springs. Then he sent Carole a bouquet of flowers with a note telling of his entry in the race.

Each day, Jim and Tennessee put the little car through new tests, and by the end of the week, they felt confident that their beetle couldn't be outrun. Still the other drivers at the track laughed at Herbie.

"What is it?" one driver said. "Something you found in a scrap heap behind Disneyland?"

"Pay no attention to them, Herbie," Tennessee told the little car. "Once the race starts, they'll know you're beautiful."

At the same time, Carole watched the little beetle through a pair of binoculars, while Thorndyke drank tea at the table he had set up near his Rolls Royce. He wondered why Carole had wanted him to take her to the races at Jackrabbit Springs.

Jackrabbit Springs was in the high California desert, and the track's lengthy uphill and downhill curves required skillful driving. Still Thorndyke had competed in the world's most difficult races, and Carole had seen many of them. Why did she want to come to Jackrabbit Springs?

Finally, just as the race started, Thorndyke said, "I'd like to know why we came down to this blazing desert?"

Carole handed him the binoculars, and he picked up the cars on the track moving from the last cars to the frontrunner — the little beetle.

"Isn't that the grubby little car we had in the shop?" Thorndyke said. "And isn't that the nasty person who bought it?"

"I think you're right," Carole said, "though I didn't think he was nasty."

Thorndyke stared angrily at Carole. In the meantime, Jim zoomed into his pit for a final stop. Tennessee speedily checked the tires. Then he poured gas into the car's tank.

"Don't make it look too easy, Herbie," Tennessee said softly. "Play it smart!"

After the pit checks were finished, Tennessee signaled Jim to take off, and the little car shot out onto the track.

Jim quickly passed several other cars in the race and eased into third place behind a Triumph and Healy battling their way toward the finish line. Then he floored the little car's gas pedal! Herbie responded, moving between the two leaders and pushing out in front of them. In the short distance that remained, the Triumph and Healy's drivers tried to get one final spurt from their cars, but Herbie refused to be overtaken.

"The winner — number fifty-three!" the track's announcer screamed into his microphone. "Jim Douglas, driving a Class D Special!"

Tennessee was grinning and jumping up and down when the little car coasted back into the pit. Helping Jim out of his seat, he said, "Herbie's the greatest thing on wheels!"

"What about me?" Jim said. "Wouldn't you say that was a fair piece of driving?"

"Sure, Jim. I didn't mean to take anything away from you."

"Tennessee, I wouldn't admit this to anyone else," Jim said seriously. "Lately, I was beginning to believe I'd never be anything. Then this starts to happen!"

"I'm glad for you," Tennessee said, glancing quickly at Herbie. "I always knew you'd make it."

Jim started to say something else, but he stopped when he saw Thorndyke and Carole. "I see you finally learned how to handle this car!" she said, while Thorndyke stared in amazement at Herbie. "Congratulations!"

Jim smiled fondly at Carole and introduced her to Tennessee.

"I think I'll take the car back and give you a thousand

dollars for yourself," Thorndyke told Jim. "What do you think of that?"

"No!" Tennessee said. "You don't want to do that, Jim!"

Jim looked smugly at the man who had sold Herbie to him. "I'm afraid Mr. Thorndyke is a little mixed up as to who — or what — won that race. Some day I'll teach him not to confuse the car with the driver."

"I should welcome a lesson from you, Douglas," Thorndyke replied.

"That's a very good idea," Carole said. "You're racing in the Riverside Libre Open at the end of the month, Mr. Thorndyke. Perhaps Jim — I mean Mr. Douglas — might enter the race. Then he could bet his share of the little car against his remaining payments."

A sly smile spread across Thorndyke's face. "Good thinking, Miss Bennett. What do you say, Mr. Douglas? The winner becomes the one and only owner of the little car?"

Tennessee tugged fearfully at his partner's arm, and Jim hesitated, wondering if the little car could hold up on the gruelling course at Riverside.

Thorndyke's smile broadened. "A moment ago you mentioned teaching me a lesson. Do I now sense that my offer to take that lesson frightens you?"

"All right, Thorndyke!" Jim said angrily. "Racing — that's the name of the game, isn't it? It's put up or shut up, so you just got yourself a bet! I'll see you at Riverside!"

Thorndyke bowed slightly and then headed for his Rolls Royce. Carole left, too, after she and Jim had once again exchanged warm smiles.

Jim's eyes followed Carole, but his thoughts were fixed on Riverside. "I'm hitting the showers, Tennessee," he said. "I'll be back in a little while."

Jim walked off, while Tennessee rubbed some of the track's dust off Herbie's front fender. He was worried. Jim expected an awful lot from his little friend, and Jim didn't give Herbie much credit for anything. "Don't mind him, little fellow," Tennessee said. "Jim might act strange at times, but he likes you. I know he does."

## IV

As THE DAYS leading to the Libre Open at Riverside passed, Tennessee's fears about the race continued to grow. Still he tried to hide his doubts from Herbie. "You'll win," he told the little car every night. "I have faith in you."

On the other hand, Jim regained much of his driving confidence. As the date for the race drew nearer, he often thought of calling Carole and thanking her for suggesting the bet that he had made with Thorndyke. Besides that, he liked her and wanted to see her again, but he wasn't sure that Carole wanted him to win the race or even wanted to hear his voice.

Carole had mixed feelings about the outcome of the race. Thorndyke had often been kind to her, and she felt a sense of responsibility to him. Still she liked Jim. She wished that he would call and help her make a decision about the race, but he didn't call.

On the track at Riverside, Carole saw Jim again. He was seated in the little car, and Tennessee was pushing it to its starting position. Jim saw her, too. She was leaning on the

back fender of Thorndyke's big Apollo Special. They nodded, each waiting for the other to smile first. Then they both turned their attentions back to the race which was about to start.

"I'm up tight," Tennessee told Jim. "Anything goes wrong, and we're liable to lose Herbie altogether."

"Don't worry," Jim replied. "You're supposed to be the one with all the faith in this car."

At the same time, Thorndyke leaned out of his Apollo and said to Carole, "Keep your eye on your friend in the bug, my dear. I'm going to squash him!"

Carole turned away, just as the track announcer said, "Clear the racing field, please! Drivers, start your engines!"

The roar of engines silenced the buzzing crowds in the stands, and, one by one, the drivers signaled to the starter that they were ready. Then he leaped high into the air, starting the race, and the rows of shiny cars leaped forward.

By the start of the third lap, Thorndyke was in the lead, and Jim, driving cautiously, but keeping within striking distance of Thorndyke's Apollo, was in ninth position.

When Thorndyke passed his pit again, he saw Carole holding up the message board. It read, "HE'S A HALF LAP BEHIND."

Grinning, Thorndyke waved to show Carole that he had gotten the message and then shot quickly past her. He almost laughed, thinking of Douglas and that little bug trying to outrun his Apollo. Oh, it was a nice little car, worth winning in a bet, but it wasn't an Apollo no matter what Douglas did to it.

While Thorndyke was daydreaming, Jim had begun to apply a little more foot pressure to Herbie's gas pedal. He rapidly passed two cars and hit the straightaway leading past the pits. Then he went out and around two more cars, before glancing over at his pit for any messages.

"NOT YET, HERBIE!" the board in Tennessee's hand read.

Jim almost couldn't believe his eyes. What made Tennessee think that it wasn't the right time to overtake Thorndyke? And what made him make the message out to the car, instead of the driver? Jim's last question was answered almost as soon as he thought of it. Herbie's engine slowed down considerably, and the car right in front of Herbie increased its lead.

Lap after lap, Thorndyke widened the distance between himself and the other cars, and at the start of the last two laps of the race, it seemed to all the spectators that no one was going to catch Thorndyke's Apollo Special. It seemed that way to Jim, too, and he wondered if he should stop at his pit and have Herbie checked out. But with two laps left, there wouldn't be time to make repairs and try to get back into the race.

Then as Jim passed his pit for the next to last time, he saw Tennessee frantically waving the message board. It read, "GO GET HIM, HERBIE!"

The little car blasted forward like a jet airliner, throwing Jim back against his seat. Seconds later, Jim was smiling and passing cars one after another. Weaving outside, then inside, then outside again, Jim finally whipped past the second place car and set his sights on Thorndyke who had just hit the straightaway and was about to pass his pit.

The happy and confident Thorndyke had eased off to almost a cruising speed, as he breezed past Carole's message, "LOOK BEHIND YOU!"

Glancing over his shoulder, he quickly spotted the trou-

53
53

ble — the little bug! He pushed his gas pedal to the floor, hoping to put many yards of racing field between himself and the bug. Jim and Herbie had other plans, though.

Seconds later, Jim steered to the outside of the course and said, "Let's give Thorndyke a look at your rear bumper, Herbie!"

The little car started past the now dusty Apollo, but Thorndyke swerved out, cutting Herbie off and causing Jim to hit his brakes. Again the little car tried to pass, and again Thorndyke cut it off.

Jim didn't mind Thorndyke's moves. They were all part of the game, but he realized he didn't have much time left to break past the Apollo. He tried again, and this time, Thorndyke swerved sharply, forcing Jim onto the road's shoulder. Jim spun out, raising a huge cloud of dust.

Seeing the cloud of dust behind him, Thorndyke figured the little car was out of the race, so he calmly settled back in his seat and coasted toward the finish line.

He didn't hear Carole calling, "Look out!" Though if he had, it still would have been too late, because the little car was alongside him and past him almost as soon as he caught sight of it. He watched sadly, as the little car went over the finish line first.

A little later, Thorndyke pushed past reporters and officials gathered together in Jim's pit and threw open Herbie's hood. "I demand this car be taken in and checked!" Thorndyke screamed, staring at Herbie's little engine. "There's more going on here than meets the eye!"

Thorndyke noticed that everybody in the pit seemed to be looking at the ground, so he looked down and saw the stream of oil that Herbie was shooting on his shoes.

## V

IN THE WEEKS that followed, Jim defeated Thorndyke in several important races, including the Mexican Road Race. Losing the Road Race really irritated Thorndyke, and for several days after the race, he angrily paced back and forth in his office.

Finally Carole told him, "You don't look too well lately."

"Of course not!" Thorndyke roared. "How could I look well? I haven't been able to sleep very much, and when I finally do get to sleep, that rotten little car drives into my dreams!"

"Did you ever think that it may not be the little car?" Carole asked. "Perhaps it's the way Jim Douglas drives."

"That's a bit of rot!" Thorndyke said, displeased by the thought. "There isn't a driver in the world can get that much speed out of a little car like that! That Douglas has done something to it, and I've got to find out what!"

As Carole started to leave the office, an idea came into Thorndyke's head, and his eyes brightened. "Carole, there's something slightly unusual that I'd like you to do for Peter

Thorndyke, Limited," he said, just as his phone rang.

It was for Carole, and she recognized Jim's voice almost immediately. He wanted to take her to dinner that night, and she, though hesitating at first, accepted. Then she put down the phone and turned to Thorndyke.

"There's something I have to tell you," she said.

"It can wait," Thorndyke replied. "I've been thinking that you should become friendly with Mr. Douglas. Who knows? Maybe he is as talented as you seem to think. If so, perhaps we can give him the opportunity to join us. He can race under our colors, but first we must know something about him."

Carole smiled. "How about tonight?"

"A splendid idea!" Thorndyke said. "In fact, take my Special. Douglas likes that car."

"Thanks, but I think I must tell you that was Mr. Douglas who called just then, and I agreed to have dinner with him before you suggested anything."

Thorndyke lifted his right arm and said, "I salute your honesty, my dear. A quality to be admired and even used, at times."

Carole returned to the agency's showroom, and Thorndyke sat down at his desk and searched the phone book for Jim Douglas' address.

A few hours later, Jim came down from his bedroom and saw Tennessee busily polishing Herbie.

"I'm not taking the little car," Jim said. "I guess I forgot to tell you that Miss Bennett called back, and she's picking me up in the Apollo."

"Herbie's been looking forward to some relaxation," Tennessee said. "And now you're not taking him?"

"I'm sorry," Jim said.

"Sorry? Is that all you can say? That's some thanks for what Herbie did for you!"

Jim heard the Apollo's horn ringing outside. "I'll see you later," he told Tennessee.

Tennessee heard the Apollo's door slam, and then heard the big car drive away. He walked over to the little car and touched its roof. "Don't let him bother you, Herbie," he said. "He doesn't mean it. Besides, he ain't the first guy to lose his head over a bucket seat and a flashy paint job. He'll come to his senses."

Minutes later, Tennessee heard a knock at the door and opened it. There stood Thorndyke. "Sorry," Tennessee said, starting to close the door. "The Board of Health is getting strict about rats on the premises."

"Oh, that's all right," Thorndyke said, smiling cleverly. "I didn't come to see Mr. Douglas. I just wanted to pay my respects to that gallant little car."

Tennessee shook his head. "I don't get you."

"Ah, there it is!" Thorndyke said, pushing his way past Tennessee and walking toward the little car. "What a marvel it is indeed! Forgive me for saying so, but it takes class to know when it has been defeated by class."

Though puzzled by the change in Thorndyke, Tennessee said, "I think I may have misjudged you, Mr. Thorndyke. I have been misjudging a lot of people lately."

"To think," Thorndyke said, touching Herbie's roof, "that this gentle, innocent little object is capable of such great deeds. How does it do it?"

"How about a drink of Irish coffee?" Tennessee said cheerfully. "It's my own mother's recipe."

"I believe I will," Thorndyke said, hoping to get a closer look at the little car, while Tennessee made the drinks.

As soon as Tennessee went off to the kitchen area, Thorndyke opened the little car's hood and searched for changes in the engine. He didn't see anything unusual, and then Tennessee returned, holding a welder's torch beneath a water kettle.

"I hope you don't mind instant coffee," Tennessee said.

Thorndyke said that instant coffee would be fine, so Tennessee blasted the kettle with his torch and then poured the steaming water into two cups. After that, he put some Irish whiskey into each of the cups and topped both drinks with a squirt of whipped cream.

"Here you go," Tennessee said, handing a cup to Thorndyke.

Thorndyke raised his cup and said, "To the little car! But may the best car win in our next race at Riverside!"

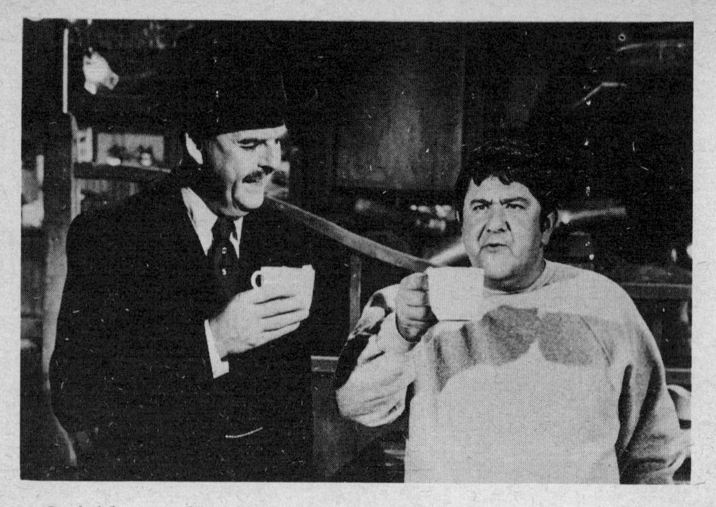

Quickly swallowing part of the drink already in his mouth, Tennessee said, "I think I'll drink to that!"

Minutes later, while Tennessee was torching another kettle of water for more rounds of Irish coffee, Jim was driving Carole to a spot she recognized right away.

"Not Seabreeze Point again!" Carole said. "Do you always drive up here after you eat?"

"This is very strange," Jim said, glancing over at Carole and smiling. "First the little car gets out of control and comes here. Now this one does the same thing."

Jim pulled into a parking space, while Carole pretended to be struggling with the door.

"Well," Jim said, as he turned off the Apollo's engine, "you seem to be locked in again, and the engine just stalled out."

Carole turned to Jim and said, "That's how it is with cars sometimes. I guess we'll wait and see what happens."

Jim wouldn't have waited to see anything, if he had any idea of what was happening back at the firehouse. Tennessee and Thorndyke were drunk, and while Tennessee prepared more drinks, his sly drinking partner poured a cupful of Irish coffee into Herbie's gas tank.

"You want to know the secret of the little car?" Tennessee called from the kitchen. "I'll tell you the secret of the little car!"

"Please tell me!" Thorndyke called back, while he squirted the rest of the whipped cream into Herbie's tank.

"It's heart!" Tennessee screamed. "That's what it is — heart!"

Thorndyke staggered into the firehouse's kitchen area and handed the empty whipped cream can to Tennessee. "We're run out, old chap," he said. "Besides that, it's late, and I should be getting home. We both have a big race ahead of us tomorrow."

"It's heart!" Tennessee screamed again.

"I'll just make a note of that before I leave," Thorndyke said, trying to balance his shaky body, while he searched for his notebook.

"Heart!" Thorndyke said. "Make a note of that before I leave!"

In the meantime, Jim had moved closer to Carole, and she said, "I've heard that Jim Douglas was only interested in big, fast cars and easy money."

"That's not true," Jim said, slipping his arm around her shoulder. "Mr. Douglas is very romantic. In fact, you want to know something?"

"What?"

"When the light hits you just right, you're as beautiful as this Apollo."

She laughed. Then they kissed. After a while, she said, "We'd better go, Jim. You have a big race tomorrow."

Starting the Apollo, Jim grinned and said, "I have heard that Carole Bennett is only interested in little cars and poor drivers."

## VI

WHEN JIM got home, he found Tennessee sound asleep inside Herbie. "Get up!" Jim said, shaking Tennessee. "Get up and go to sleep in your bed!"

It was no use. Tennessee wouldn't budge, so Jim went up to bed for a quick nap before they had to load the beetle into the truck for its long ride to Riverside Raceway. He was disappointed. He wanted to tell his roommate how much he liked Carole, but that would have to wait.

On the way to Riverside, Tennessee was quiet, so Jim said, "What's bothering you?"

"It's Herbie," Tennessee said. "The little car has feelings, and you have to start thinking about it."

"All right," Jim said, "I will. But for now, let's think about today's race."

Tennessee and Jim talked very little after that, but just before the start of the race Jim said, "There's something wrong here. Listen to that motor. It doesn't have the old zing."

"Stop worrying," Tennessee said, frowning. "You think Herbie would let you down?"

Jim glanced over to Thorndyke's pit and saw Carole. Her attention was on Thorndyke who was almost ready to climb into the red Ferrari he would be driving. For a man who had taken an aspirin less than half an hour before, he seemed very cheerful.

"Is your headache gone?" Carole asked.

"Of course, my dear," Thorndyke replied, looking over at Herbie and then grinning. "Today is my day. All my big and *little* headaches are taken care of."

Puzzled, Carole said, "You seem extra confident today."

"Yes, I believe I am," Thorndyke said, and then he climbed into his Ferrari.

When the race started, Thorndyke jumped into the lead, but Jim twisted Herbie past the Ferrari on the first curve and held first place at the end of the opening lap.

He held his lead for several more laps and seemed to be on his way to another victory, until Herbie hiccoughed. Then the little car hiccoughed again and again, and its little body bounced up and down, while Jim hung on to the little car's wheel to keep from being hiccoughed through its roof.

Thorndyke whizzed past the troubled little car. Then several other cars also passed, while Herbie weaved all over the track.

"Come in!" Tennessee's signboard read, as Herbie staggered by.

A blob of foam spurted out of Herbie's exhaust pipe and onto the signboard. Tennessee looked at it. The foam looked familiar, so he smelled it. Finally, he tasted it. "Irish coffee!" he called angrily. "That dirty Thorndyke!"

Meanwhile, Carole couldn't believe Herbie's performance on the track. What was wrong with the little car? It

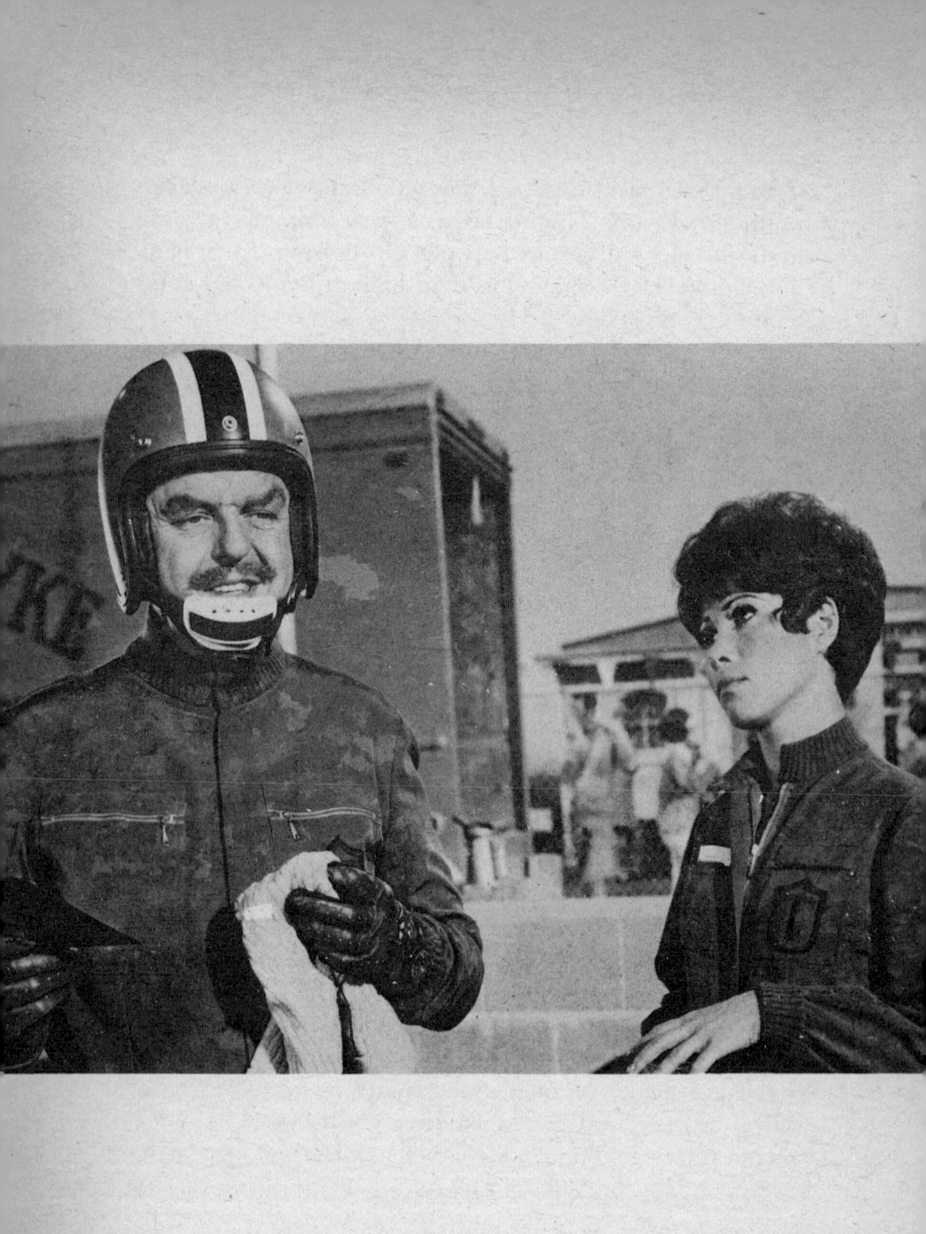

seemed as if it was drunk. Then she thought of Thorndyke's headache. Where had he been the night before? Why had he been so anxious to let her use the Apollo?

When Thorndyke came into the pit for a refueling, Carole said, "Did you go to Mr. Douglas' garage last night?"

"Yes, I did," Thorndyke said, slightly surprised by her question. "In fact, I had a most delightful evening."

"So while I was having dinner with Mr. Douglas, you were messing with his car! Is that correct?"

Thorndyke got the signal from his mechanic and started his engine. "All things are possible!" he called over the roar of the engine. "After the race, my dear, we'll celebrate!"

Carole watched him drive away. He was going to win the race, but he was going to have to do his celebrating alone. She took one last sad glance at Herbie, weakly trying to finish the race. Then she looked around for a ride back to San Francisco.

After Thorndyke was awarded the winner's trophy, newsmen asked him to pose by the Ferrari. Thorndyke smiled smugly, while the photographers raced around, taking shots of him and the car from different angles.

Nearby, Tennessee was driving Herbie up the ramp into the truck that had carried the little car to the race. Suddenly, Herbie hiccoughed and fired a blob of whipped cream at Thorndyke! Then Herbie hiccoughed again and again, aiming one blob of whipped cream after another at Thorndyke. Finally, the last hiccoughed blob landed on Thorndyke's face, while the photographers clicked away.

That evening, Tennessee was alone with the little car. "Don't worry, Herbie," he said. "Jim will be back any minute now. He wouldn't have left you in this condition, if it hadn't been something important."

Then he heard a knock at the firehouse door. He slid it open, expecting to see Jim on the other side.

"May I come in?" Carole said. "Though I wouldn't blame you if you threw me out."

"On account of what Thorndyke did?" Tennessee asked, stepping aside to let her enter. "How can I blame anyone? Thorndyke made Herbie sick right under my nose."

Looking around, Carole said, "Where's Jim?"

"He went out soon as we got back. Never said a word. Left Herbie and me flat. Say, you know something about mechanics? I mean car fixing, not men."

"A little," Carole said. "Why?"

"Well, maybe you can help the little car," Tennessee said. "I'm not a mechanic, but I think it's suffering."

"Suffering?"

"Yeah. Herbie don't feel good. Not that you'd ever hear him complain."

Tennessee got a set of coveralls and held them out to Carole.

"All right," she said. "But I do want you to know I'm not with Peter Thorndyke anymore. I don't think his way."

"I know that."

Smiling, Carole stepped into the coveralls. Then she started to work on Herbie's engine. She had been around cars most of her life and was a good mechanic, yet most men didn't want to believe that. She looked fondly at Tennessee. They had met a few times at different tracks, but they somehow had become friends. She could feel it.

Tennessee felt the same friendly feeling coming over him, and he needed her friendship. "I've got to level with someone!" he said desperately. "I can't talk to Jim. It would destroy him!"

"Destroy him?" she repeated.

Tennessee moved closer to her. "You don't know what it was like before this little car come along. Jim couldn't keep a job. He got into trouble all the time. Everyone was on his back. Then Herbie come into his life. You remember that day?"

"I remember," Carole said.

"Jim starts winning races. He gets his self-respect back. So what am I going to do? Keep telling him that it's Herbie winning those races?"

"What makes you think it was Herbie?" Carole said. "Jim's a fine driver."

"You ever hear of a place called Tibet?"

"Yes."

"Well, you must know about those mountains that got monks and swamis and gurus on top of them. So you go ahead and fix the little car, while I tell you what's going on."

Carole cleared the fuel lines. After that, she cleaned the sparkplugs and checked out the wiring, and Tennessee explained about how he plugged in on contemplation. Then she started Herbie's engine and said, "How's that?"

Tennessee looked joyful. "It's like the sound of one hand clapping. Herbie and I sure appreciate it."

Carole smiled. Then she shot a puzzled glance at the little car.

"You don't believe what I told you about Herbie?" Tennessee said.

"Well," Carole said, searching for the right words, "there's always a first time. I imagine Adam thought Woman was a pretty funny piece of equipment when he met Eve."

"Good!" Tennessee said. "You don't have to believe it all right away. It takes time. Now is there anything else we should do for Herbie?"

"He could use a washing, but do you think Jim will think doing all this is all right?"

"Don't worry," Tennessee said. "Jim will be real happy that you're here."

"I hope you're right," Carole whispered, almost to herself.

## VII

CAROLE AND TENNESSEE were washing the little car in the courtyard, when Jim drove up in a sleek, new red Ferrari. He got out and stood a few feet from the new car, admiring it.

"What's this thing?" Tennessee said, snapping Jim out of the trance he seemed to be in.

Jim noticed Carole and said, "Hi. How do you like my new car?"

"Very nice," she said.

"Say, what's the big idea?" Tennessee said angrily. "You already got a car!"

"Not after what happened today," Jim said. "The El Dorado is coming up soon, and I need a car that can cut it."

"What are you talking about?" Tennessee fumed. "Herbie cut it so far, didn't he?"

"Of course it has!" Carole added.

"Listen," Jim told them, "I've done great with this little car so far. Thanks to changes I made. Also, if you don't mind, thanks to some pretty fair driving! But I had to stop kidding myself. I needed a strong car. Now I got it!"

The phone sounded inside the firehouse, and Jim, excusing himself, rushed in to get the call. It was Thorndyke, calling from the phone in his car. Jim warned Thorndyke that he knew what had happened to Herbie.

"You can't imagine how I feel," Thorndyke said, pausing momentarily to frame his next sentence. "I'm simply not myself when I've been drinking. Haven't you ever had too much?"

"I'll think about that and call you back in a few years," Jim said.

"Don't hang up!" Thorndyke said. "I heard you bought a Ferrari today and that you owe quite a bit of money on it. Myself, I like the little car, and I'm willing to give you fifteen hundred dollars for it right now. I'm near your neighborhood."

"Thorndyke, I don't like you, but I can use your money," Jim said. "So come and get your little car."

Tennessee and Carole walked in, just as Jim put down the phone. "I'm selling the little car," he said. "I need the money."

"You crumb!" Tennessee screamed. "You're not doing that to Herbie!"

"I don't want to believe you'd do something like this to Herbie!" Carole added.

"Has everyone gone nuts around here? Carole, I can understand how Tennessee feels. He's just in off a flying saucer, but I thought you made sense."

Carole frowned. "I don't care what I made. I do know that it's wrong to sell that little car."

"This is funny," Jim said, forcing himself to smile. "You

go out with me last night, while your boss works on the little car, and now you tell me not to sell it."

"Is that what you think?" Carole asked.

"Well, it's a tempting idea."

"If you must know, I'm through with Thorndyke, because of what he did," Carole said. "But I think it's about time someone told you what the score is. Tennessee's too kind. You really think it was you winning those races?"

"Wait a minute!" Tennessee said to Carole. "Don't send him down the tubes yet!"

"Shut up!" Jim warned, turning to Carole. "Now you go ahead and clue me in!"

Tennessee angrily walked off to the kitchen and poured himself a cup of cold coffee.

Carole moved closer to Jim. "All right, windbag," she said, "I'll tell you something. Your head's all swelled up because you think you're winning those races! Well, you're not winning any of them! You couldn't win a foot race with a fish!"

Jim stopped and listened to the sound of metal scraping and banging coming from outside. It got louder, as he listened. Finally, he called, "Tennessee, stop that noise out there!"

"I'm not out there, crumb!" Tennessee called from the kitchen. "I'm here!"

Terror seized Jim. He ran outside as fast as he could, with Carole and Tennessee right after him. Then he saw it. Herbie was banging into the side of the Ferrari. Jim was too late, though, because the Ferrari looked like a soggy waffle. He turned and grabbed a broom that was leaning against the fence. Then he went after Herbie.

"Stop it!" Tennessee said, throwing his arms around Jim.

"Do you hear me? You don't know what you're doing."

Jim sagged in Tennessee's arms and then said weakly, "You see what it's done?"

"Just calm down," Tennessee said. "Herbie lost his head. So maybe he was jealous."

"Sure it's jealous," Jim said. "It never could stand it when I got credit for winning those races!"

Jim paused, realizing what he was saying. Then he sat down, trying to think about what was happening to him. Before Jim could think it all out, Thorndyke pulled up and climbed out of his car.

"Here," he said, waving a check at Jim. "Whatever is going on here, I always say that money serves to ease the pain. Here's your fifteen hundred dollars, as I promised."

No one said a word, and this puzzled Thorndyke even more. He quickly wrote another check. "Two!" he said. "How about two thousand dollars? The least I can do to help a fellow human at a time like this!"

Slowly raising his head, Jim said, "Two thousand dollars for this beat up little car. Why, Thorndyke?"

"I've always had a warm place in my heart for the little thing."

"You don't have a warm place on your entire body!" Jim said. "Now what do you want it for?"

"You don't want it. I do, so take the money."

Jim stood up and grabbed Thorndyke by his coat lapels. "Why do you want it?"

"I'm just trying to give you some money," Thorndyke said.

"No, you believe it, too! I can tell!"

"What difference does it make?" Tennessee said softly. "Herbie don't believe in you no more, Jim."

Turning to answer Tennessee, Jim saw that the little car wasn't in the courtyard. "Where is it?" he mumbled, suddenly feeling guilty about the Ferrari and other things that might've prompted the little car's disappearance.

"Took off," Tennessee said sadly. "What did you expect?"

It was late. Where would Herbie go alone at night? All along, Jim had hoped that some very simple mechanical fact would explain the little car's unusual actions. Now he knew that Tennessee had been close to the truth right from the start. "Come on!" Jim pleaded. "Help me go after it!"

Tennessee shook his head. "No. This is a private thing — between the two of you."

Jim ran into the street and looked both ways. The car wasn't in sight. Then he started down the hill, and his body soon faded into darkness. At the same time, Thorndyke got back into his car and picked up the phone. "Operator," he said, "give me 489-8458. . . . Havershaw, I shall require every man on our staff. We have a small task to perform right now."

While Thorndyke outlined his plans to Havershaw, Jim continued through street after street, calling, "Herbie! Herbie, come on back!"

A little later, though Jim didn't know it, Thorndyke's tow trucks entered the search for Herbie. On foot, Jim was no match for the trucks, and one of them soon found the little car. The truck's driver quickly slipped two hooks under Herbie's rear axle and then towed the little car to the alley behind Thorndyke's showroom.

Thorndyke met the truck by the entrance to his workshop. "Good work," he told the driver. "Now get it inside and tell Havershaw to get some torches heated up. Once and for all we're going to find out what makes this little thing tick."

A sinister grin spread across Thorndyke's face, as he watched the little car roll into his workshop. He quickly glanced up and down the dark alley. Then he stepped inside his building.

## VIII

A FLAMING RAGE grew within Thorndyke as he eyed the little car and thought of the newspaper story he had seen about his victory at Riverside. He angrily recalled the photo of himself after the race and the caption under it — "Thorndyke Wins Cup at Riverside, and Douglas Car Supplies Cream!"

"Even when I win, you make a fool of me," Thorndyke cried, kicking savagely at Herbie's rear bumper.

Suddenly, as if awakened by Thorndyke's foot, the little car's engine started with a loud roar. Thorndyke stood there in shock, not wanting to believe his ears or eyes, until one of Herbie's rear tires backed over his feet.

"Get it!" Thorndyke screamed, hopping after Herbie. "Get that little monster!"

The little car managed to back into the showroom, before Thorndyke and his men crowded it into a corner. Then the men moved in on Herbie, and the little car shifted into low and shot past them and through the showroom's plate glass window into the street. Thorndyke and

TER THORNDYKE
ORTED EUROPEAN MO
53

his men followed, but by the time they had eased themselves through the broken glass, Herbie was gone.

Grinning, one of Thorndyke's men said, "Man, that little thing's out of sight!"

"That's a brilliant observation!" Thorndyke said, and then he marched back into his showroom.

Meanwhile, Jim had reached the edge of the city's Chinatown section in his search for Herbie. He wondered whether he should go on, when the little car spun around a corner.

"Herbie!" Jim called. "Where have you been?"

The little car still didn't want to see Jim, and it raced wildly in the opposite direction, smashing into the side of a store, just before it turned another corner. Mr. Tang Wu, the store's owner, got a good look at the little car with the number "53" on it, before the car and the man running after it disappeared.

About half an hour later, Herbie rolled up to one of the Golden Gate Bridge's toll booths. The fog was so heavy that the man in the booth almost didn't see the little car. As he held out his hand for the toll, he bent down to take a look at the driver. Then he glanced quickly at the fog blanketing the bridge. It was the first fog he could remember that completely covered a car's driver. He bent down again to look for the little car's driver, but this time the little car raced off down the bridge.

The man quickly picked up the phone in his booth and phoned the police on the other side of the bridge, telling them to watch for a little car that had gotten on the bridge without paying.

Seconds later, Jim dragged himself up to the booth and said, "Did a little car just come by here?"

"Yes," the man in the booth said. "But it'll be back. It's

driver must have thought that he could avoid the toll fee."

Drawing new energy from his weary body, Jim, too, raced down the bridge without paying. Near the middle of the bridge, he saw Herbie. The little car had driven its front wheels over the bridge railing and was racing its engine, trying to get its rear wheels to throw it into the waters below.

"No, Herbie!" Jim cried. "Please don't!"

First Jim grabbed the little car's rear bumper and tried to pull the little car back to safety. It was no use, so he worked his way around to the front of the car. Then Jim slipped and had to take hold of Herbie's front bumper to keep from falling into the Bay. There, swinging back and forth over the water, Jim realized that he was in danger.

"Help me!" he called. "Herbie, help me!"

Jim's plea seemed to awaken the little car, and it dropped its rear wheels down onto the bridge. Then Herbie's spinning rear wheels seemed to flip the front wheels over the railing to safety. Jim came over the railing, too, and struck his head on the bridge's driving surface. The blow knocked him unconscious, just as two policemen came out of the fog and toward him.

"Was that guy lucky!" one policeman said. "That little car saved his life!"

The other policeman didn't want to believe what his partner had said. "You must be kidding?" he said. "You really don't believe that the little car saved his life, do you?"

"Well, that's what it looked like," the first policeman said. "You know how funny things look in the fog sometimes."

Shaking his head, the other policeman said, "Personally,

I think you've been around too many hippies lately. The car saved his life. Buddy, you save that kind of talk for your hippie pals."

"All right!" the first policeman said. "So I made a mistake! Listen, you see if you can wake this guy, while I split. I mean, while I go to the car and call in. A little car like this did some damage in Chinatown about an hour ago."

The other policeman laughed. "Do you know how many other little cars there are like this?"

"With a number '53' painted on them?" the first policeman asked and then went off to call in about Herbie.

A little later, Tennessee walked into the police station garage and spotted Jim. "What's all the trouble?" Tennessee asked.

"Do you see that Chinese gentleman standing over there by Herbie?" Jim said. "Well, Herbie smashed into his store and did a lot of damage. Now, Mr. Wu, that's the man's name, wants money to repair the damage, or Herbie gets sold at a police auction, and the money goes to Mr. Wu."

Tennessee smiled. "Let me talk to the gentleman," he said. "My guru taught me Chinese, and I taught him English when we were on the mountain."

Jim followed Tennessee over to Mr. Wu, wondering if Tennessee really knew Chinese. He had said it, and within moments, he and Mr. Wu were wandering around Herbie and talking very quickly and friendly—in Chinese. Then Mr. Wu pulled a magazine from inside his coat. It was a car racing magazine that Jim immediately recognized. Except, the writing on it was Chinese.

"What's going on?" Jim said to Tennessee.

"He's a racing car fan," Tennessee said. "He was just telling me about some of Herbie's winning races. Now

there's only one problem. I think he wants to keep Herbie for himself."

"Wait!" Jim said. "I think we can make a deal. We give him Herbie, if he lets me drive the little car in the El Dorado. Then if we win, Mr. Wu gets all of the prize money."

"All of the prize money?" Tennessee repeated, trying to understand Jim's deal.

"Right," Jim said. "But if we win, he has to sell Herbie back to us for one dollar."

Tennessee felt tears forming in the corners of his eyes, and he held them back, asking, "You'd do that for Herb?"

Jim grinned and slapped his chubby friend's back. "You tell Mr. Wu. I'll listen."

When Tennessee finished explaining about the El Dorado, Mr. Wu turned to Jim and bowed. "All of a sudden," he said in clear English, "you turn me on."

Then the two of them shook hands, sealing their agreement.

"I'll walk Mr. Wu to his car," Tennessee said. "I'll be right back."

After Tennessee and Mr. Wu had gone, Jim turned to the little car. "Well, it's all up to you, Herbie," he said, gently patting its roof.

## IX

JIM, CAROLE, and Tennessee entered the El Dorado Hotel's crowded press headquarters one week after Mr. Wu had become Herbie's new owner. They were there to hear the President of the Southwestern Racing Association offer some final thoughts about the race before it started.

After they found seats, Carole said, "Where's Thorndyke?"

"That's funny," Jim said. "I was just about to ask you the same question. I noticed a few of his mechanics down front, but I don't see him."

"There he is," Tennessee said, pointing to Thorndyke talking to some newspaper reporters near the back of the room. "He's probably telling them how great he is."

Then the Racing Association President entered the room, and it became very quiet. Everyone rose, partly in respect for the President who had once been a great driver, and partly because each of them knew the days, weeks, and months of planning and talking about the rugged El Dorado were about to end. In a short while, both cars

and drivers would be showing what they had — or what they needed.

Breaking through the anxious silence that filled the room, the President said, "You will follow the route which has been posted for this race. Other than that, we're putting the emphasis on speed, endurance, and courage. You may use any style of car and any crew you please. The object, ladies and gentlemen, is to win! So I wish all of you the best of luck!"

The meeting was over, and after some short enthusiastic applause, the owners, drivers, and crews made their way to the exits, except for Thorndyke. He found Mr. Wu and led him by the arm to the side of the room.

"I understand, sir, you are now the owner of the little Douglas car?" Thorndyke said, and Mr. Wu nodded. "Well, if you'll forgive me, sir, I must say that you are perhaps not as green as you look."

"I suppose not," Mr. Wu said.

"As a matter of fact, sir," Thorndyke continued, "you are a very clever operator, I have been told. You have managed to acquire a number of different businesses."

Bowing slightly, Mr. Wu said, "It is truly written that you cannot lose them all."

"Perhaps you believe in the little car enough to make a sizeable wager — a bet — on the outcome of the race?" Thorndyke said.

"What would you like?" Mr. Wu said, bowing again.

"For a start," Thorndyke suggested, "perhaps you could put up the little car against something of mine that you might be interested in."

While Thorndyke and Wu made their wager, Tennessee was under Herbie, taking a final look at its frame.

"How do things look under there?" Carole called, and Tennessee rolled out from under Herbie and got to his feet.

"Well," he said hesitatingly, "I hope everything holds together."

Puzzled, Carole asked, "What holds together?"

"Herbie," Tennessee said, doubtfully shaking his head. "Maybe I shouldn't have done it, but Herbie's frame was all out of shape. So I cut it to get it straight again. Herbie didn't seem to mind, though."

"Well, I hope that's a good sign," Carole said, seeing Jim coming toward her and Tennessee. "But let's keep all of this a secret between you and me for now. Jim's going to have enough to worry about."

Jim nodded to Carole and Tennessee. Then he walked slowly around the little car. "Herbie looks fine," Jim said. "Let's mount up!"

First, Tennessee loaded his tools, torch, and spare parts for Herbie into the back seat. Then he got in. Jim adjusted his helmet and chin strap and climbed behind the steering wheel, smiling at Carole who was sliding into the seat next to him.

"Oh, look at what's coming over here!" Tennessee said, groaning loudly when he had finished speaking.

It was Thorndyke. "Is this an ambulance?" he said, looking in at Tennessee who continued to groan.

Jim grinned. "Thorndyke, this little car would fly, if there weren't three of us inside just to hold it on the road!"

"Three of you?" Thorndyke said, glancing into the back seat again. "Say, that's right, isn't it? He only counts for one."

"Very funny!" Tennessee called, as Thorndyke rushed off to his car and crew. "Once the race starts, I'll be waving through the back window to you!"

Minutes later, Thorndyke and his only passenger, Havershaw, sat in the front line waiting for the race to start. "Havershaw," Thorndyke said, "while we honest folk were listening to our good Racing Association President, I trust that you weren't wasting you time."

"No indeed, sir," Havershaw said, grinning and hoping that Thorndyke wanted him to grin. "I spent a few useful moments with the little car."

"From what you now know, what chance has the little car of winning this race, Havershaw?"

"Well," Havershaw said, grinning broadly, "if the other cars in the race suddenly disappeared, the little car would have a slight chance, if it could finish the race."

Thorndyke also grinned broadly. "My friend," he said, "you are a rat after my own heart!"

"Gentlemen, start your engines!" the Association President announced.

Rows and rows of cars fired their engines and waited for the signal that would send the first row racing off, followed by rows of determined pursuers.

Then the starter dropped the green flag! They were off! Thorndyke quickly jumped ahead of the other cars in the first row. Then other rows of cars rolled past the starting line and began to separate.

Jim, although he had slammed down Herb's gas pedal, seemed to be left at the gate, and the crowd near the starting line watched and wondered about the little car. Suddenly, Herbie reared back like a bucking horse, dropped to the ground again, and was off like a bolt of lightning.

53

Weaving in and out, Jim rapidly passed the cars that had been in his row. Then he overtook so many cars that they seemed to be sliding back to him. Tennessee and Carole sat there and watched without saying a word, and Jim noticed that they, especially Tennessee, seemed dazed.

"Are you all right?" Jim said, twisting slightly toward the back seat.

"Don't pay any attention to me," Tennessee warned. "At certain speeds, the wind gets in my ears, and I can't move my head."

Then Carole awakened, saying, "Jim you're doing wonderful. I think you've passed everyone but Thorndyke. He must have taken a tremendous lead."

"Look!" Jim said, pointing at Thorndyke's yellow car a few hundred feet in front of them. "Let's eat him up, Herbie!"

At the same time, Havershaw looked back and saw the little car coming up quickly. "It's almost up to us," he said.

"How wonderful," Thorndyke cheerfully commented. "Mr. Douglas is going to try to pass us on this rather hazardous mountain road. Well, we're not too concerned, are we?"

For a moment, Havershaw was puzzled. Then he glanced at a special leather flap on the floor and smiled slyly. "Concerned?" he said. "Of course not, Mr. Thorndyke."

# X

"Come on, Herbie!" Tennessee called above the roar of the little car's engine. "Pass him!"

"Here we go!" Jim said, pulling within a few feet of the Apollo's rear bumper.

Thorndyke eyed the little car in his rear view mirror and smiled. "Havershaw," he said, "aren't we coming to that rather dangerous oily spot in the road?"

"Coming right up, sir!"

Havershaw reached down and lifted the special leather flap on the floor, revealing an oil pump handle. He jerked the handle up and down a few times and then quickly glanced out of the Apollo's rear window. He spotted the oil that he had pumped onto the road a moment before and laughed out loud.

Again, Thorndyke glanced into his rear view mirror, but this time he saw the little car just as it hit the oil slick and skidded out of control.

"Havershaw, you did very well," he said, glancing around for a last look at the little beetle.

53

Meanwhile, Herbie couldn't come out of the skid and rocketed over an embankment and down a steep hill. Then while Jim struggled to regain control of the car's wheel, Tennessee watched, unable to talk and unable to close his mouth.

When Thorndyke's last look at the beetle ended, he turned and found himself on a curve that he had not expected. He frantically spun the wheel, but it was too late, and he, Havershaw and the Apollo started over the embankment. The car quickly plunged to the bottom of the hill and into a stream.

"Give it the gas, sir!" Havershaw called. "We can make it!"

From one end of the stream to the bank on the other end, the Apollo churned its way through the muddy waters, but its wheels sunk in the heavy mud on the bank. The Apollo was stuck.

Turning to Havershaw, Thorndyke said scornfully, "Give it the gas, sir. We can make it. First you fail to warn me about the curve, and now you get me stuck in this mud. Well, don't sit there looking at an idiot. I mean looking *like* an idiot. Get out and push!"

"All right," Havershaw said. "You're the boss."

He waded around to the back of the Apollo and pushed, while Thorndyke raced the engine, hoping the car would push itself out of the mud. Then Havershaw heard an engine and looked across the stream. It was the little car, bouncing its way through the woods toward the stream.

"Do you see what I see?" Carole asked Jim.

"Yes," he said, "and do you see what's on the other side of the stream—your old friend Thorndyke. Hang on! I think Herbie wants to get a closer look at the Apollo."

53
53

Herbie skipped across the water like a hockey puck crosses ice. It came alongside the Apollo in four skips. Then Jim steered it up the bank, and Herbie's rear wheels fired a barrage of mud bombs back through the Apollo's open window and into Thorndyke's face.

Herbie continued on in the search for a paved roadway, while Jim, Carole and Tennessee shook with laughter at the thought of Thorndyke's muddy face.

"Havershaw! Havershaw!" Thorndyke screamed. "Where are you? I want you to look at me!"

Havershaw, who had been knocked into the stream by one of Herbie's mud bombs, climbed out of the water and walked over to Thorndyke.

"You look absolutely charming, Mr. Thorndyke," he said. "Will there be anything else?"

"Get in the car," Thorndyke said. "I think we can rock our way out of here now, so let's try."

Five minutes later, the Apollo was on the trail that Herbie had blazed, and five minutes after that, the Apollo was back on a paved road and in the race.

Carole shot an admiring look in Jim's direction. "Herbie's a great car," she said, "and you're a great driver."

"I second and third that," Tennessee added.

Jim grinned and said, "What's going on here? Why all this unexpected praise?"

"It's partly because we're leading in this race," Carole said, "and it's partly because we like you. Is that right, Tennessee?"

"I second and third that," Tennessee said. "And Herbie fourths it."

While Herbie's passengers enjoyed their lead in the race, Thorndyke told Havershaw, "If we're where you say

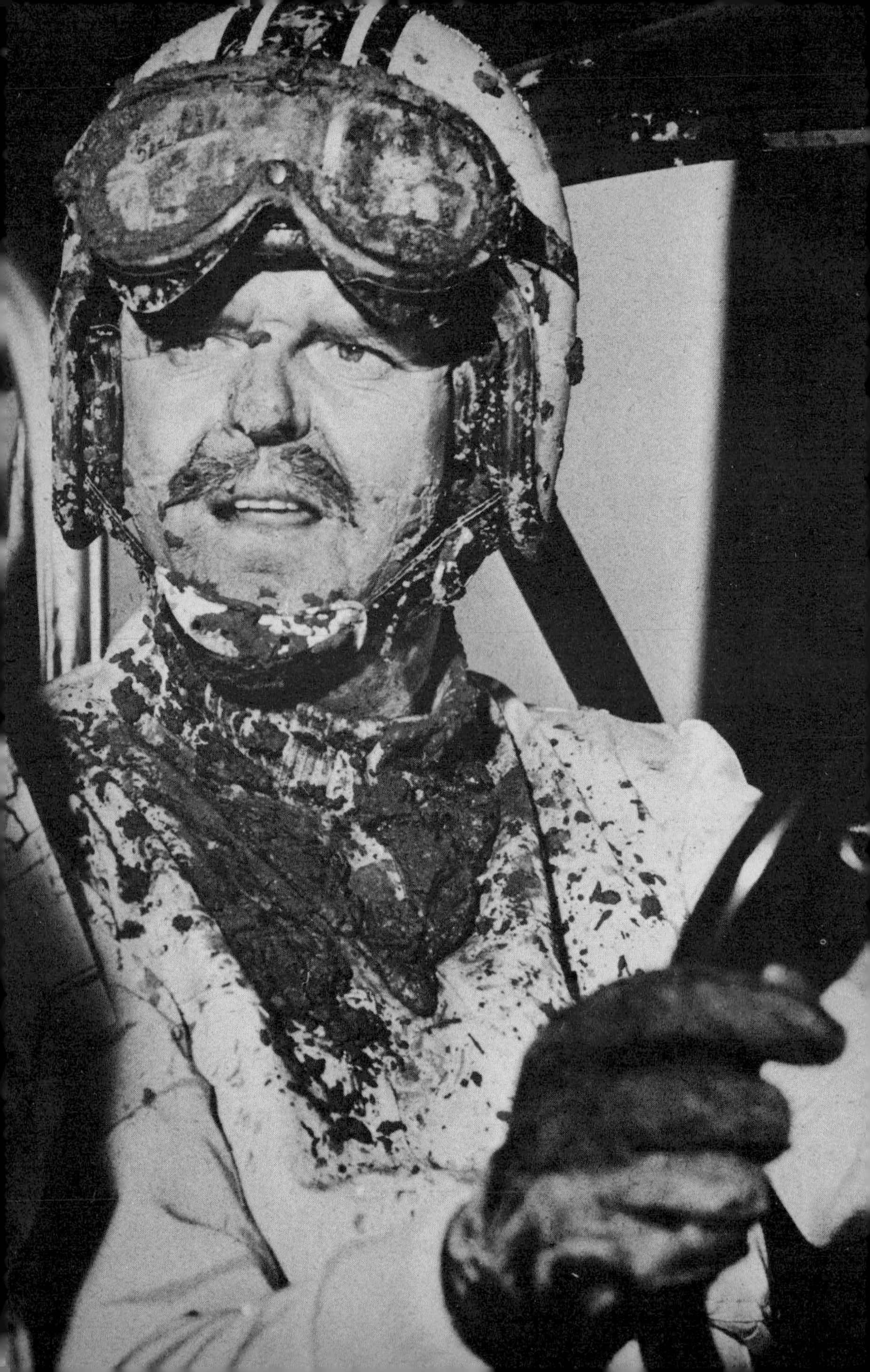

we are on that map, we have a good chance of overtaking the little car, before we or it reaches the gas station at Chinese Camp. If we're really lucky, the little car may need to be towed into Chinese Camp."

Havershaw laughed. "There's no tow truck at Chinese Camp."

"How did you guess?" Thorndyke said, chuckling to himself.

A few minutes later, Jim pulled Herbie over to the side of the road and said, "I was hoping we'd make it to Chinese Camp before gassing up again, but the needle's riding right on 'empty' so maybe we'd better fill up now."

Carole opened her door and leaned forward, allowing Tennessee to climb out. He opened the beetle's trunk and lifted out the emergency gas tank. Then he placed a funnel in the car's gas tank and poured the gas. Herbie's engine started missing. Then it sputtered as if it were out of gas. Then it stopped.

Jim jumped from the car and said, "Stop! What are you pouring in there?"

"Gas," Tennessee said, turning the tank upright. "What's the matter?"

"Smell it," Jim said sadly. "I have a hunch that Thorndyke has been up to one of his miserable tricks again."

Tennessee poured some of the liquid onto his hand and sniffed the hand. Then he licked his fingers.

"It smells like nothing," he said, "but it tastes like water."

Jim started to say something, but just then the Apollo raced by, blasting its horns at the little car and its passengers stuck on the side of the road.

"Make a note of my odometer reading," Thorndyke told

Havershaw. "When we reach Chinese Camp, let me know how far they are from it."

Two minutes later, Thorndyke pulled into the famous old mining town of Chinese Camp, and Havershaw said, "Three miles! They're stuck three miles from here!"

After fitting a nozzle into the Apollo's gas tank, an old Chinese man walked around to the side of the car and said to Thorndyke, "Where little car that always beat this car?"

"Little car out of gas three miles down the road," Thorndyke said, smiling fiendishly. "Put that in your water pipe and smoke it!"

The old man smiled politely and then yelled something in Chinese to an even older man sitting inside the gas station. The older man then got up and disappeared into the back of the station.

"I'm in a hurry," Thorndyke said. "Can't you pump that gas into my tank a little faster than that?"

The old man again smiled politely. Then he walked back to the gas pump.

## XI

JIM, CAROLE and Tennessee stared intently at their map, trying to figure out how far they were from Chinese Camp. They were so concerned that they didn't see or hear the twelve young men who came from the bushes alongside the road carrying two long, metal poles. Then the car seemed to rise from the ground, and its three riders saw the young men carrying them and the little car.

"Look!" Jim said. "They're wearing Tang Wu's Athletic Club sweatshirts, so they must be on our side."

"Well, why aren't they staying on the road?" Carole said, opening Herbie's sunroof and standing. "It may be another one of Thorndyke's tricks."

Jim stood also and called to the men in front of the car, "Where are we going?"

"Don't sweat, Douglas," a Chinese man in front of the car said. "This is Uncle Wu's car, and he's not going to let Thorndyke put him down."

About that time, Thorndyke wondered what was happening. The old man had taken a seat by his gas tank and

53
TANG WU
ATHLETIC CLUB

the pump seemed to be going, but the needle on Thorndyke's gas gauge hadn't moved.

"Can you see how much gas we've taken so far?" Thorndyke asked.

"Yes," Havershaw said.

"Well, how much?" Thorndyke screamed.

"I can see the numbers," Havershaw explained, "but they're in Chinese."

"Come on!" Thorndyke called to the old man. "I'm in a hurry!"

The old man calmly removed the nozzle from the tank and walked around to the side of the car. "Hurry is waste," he said. "Waste is cracked bowl, which never knows rice."

"I don't want a bowl of cracked rice!" Thorndyke roared. "I want . . ."

He paused, as the young men rushed past and placed Herbie next to one of the pumps. Then like lightning, they worked on the little car, filling it with gas, checking its tires and battery, cleaning the windows, and rubbing the road dust off it.

"Hey!" Thorndyke screamed. "Some of you people get over here right now!"

"Thank you so much!" Carole called, and the little car raced off.

Thorndyke started his engine, and again the old man walked around to the side of the car. "Not full," he said. "You can't go yet."

"You just watch me!" Thorndyke warned.

Thorndyke slammed down his gas pedal, and the Apollo started forward. Then it suddenly stopped, almost jerking Thorndyke and Havershaw out of their seats. They looked and saw a heavy old chain attached to the

Apollo's bumper. The other end of the chain was linked to the wall of the gas station's repair shop.

"Can't go yet," the old man said again and returned to his seat by the gas tank.

When Thorndyke finally zoomed away from the Chinese Camp gas station, Jim should have held a commanding lead. Instead, Herbie seemed to be having some engine trouble, and Jim was hoping that the little car had enough energy to make it over the steep, winding mountain road into Virginia City. There all cars and drivers had to make an overnight stop, so Jim and his partners would have some time to try to fix Herbie's engine.

"Win or lose," Jim said, "we can't blame Herbie, the greatest little car in the world."

"Herbie, the greatest?" Tennessee said, smiling at Carole. "Did I hear him right?"

Jim laughed. "Kid me all you want. It just took me some time to get over my illness."

"Illness?" Carole said jokingly. "What was wrong with you?"

"I'm not sure," Jim said, "but the sting of a four-wheeled beetle cured me."

Then the three of them laughed, unaware that Thorndyke was two hundred yards behind them.

"If your rear bumper hooks his front left wheel," Havershaw said, "he'll lose that wheel."

"Hang on," Thorndyke said, stomping down on the gas, "and for your sake, hope that those young fellows back at Chinese Camp didn't fix that loose wheel for Douglas."

When the little car's three passengers saw the Apollo coming up alongside them, they knew the little car couldn't fight back at that moment. Still they didn't expect the Apollo to brush against Herbie, but things like that did happen on narrow roads, and Thorndyke was past them before they could protest.

Then Tennessee said, "Hey! Where'd that wheel come from?"

The three of them watched the single small wheel running in front of them, until it hit the side of the road and disappeared into the gorge below. Suddenly, Herbie's left front axle bit into the ground, and Herbie's scrambled passengers identified the mysterious wheel that had bounced into the gorge.

"I can't stop!" Jim said. "If I try and Herbie turns over, we might go over the cliff. Tennessee, you get out the front door! Carole, you hold him! We'll try to balance the car like a sailboat, until it's safe to stop."

As other cars still in the race roared by, their drivers stared in amazement at the little car rolling on three wheels, while one of its passengers was halfway out of the roof holding onto another passenger who was hanging out of the window.

Jim's balancing act worked, until the car hit a stretch of level roadway, and Tennessee's weight shifted. Then Herbie was up on two wheels, but still running.

"Hold tight!" Jim called, reaching for Carole's belt. He pulled her into the car, and Tennessee's hand and arm came through the roof with her. Then the car came down hard on its front axle, flipping the rest of Tennessee's body through the roof and into Herbie's back seat. This time, the car stopped completely, and the other front wheel broke loose and started down the road by itself.

Jim leaped from his driver's seat and started after the

53

wheel. As it reached the edge of the road, Jim dived for it, but the wheel went over the cliff. For a moment, Jim merely watched the wheel as it bounced and tumbled into the rocks and trees below. Then Carole and Tennessee slid to the ground beside Jim.

"What are we going to do now?" Carole said.

"I don't know," Jim said. "We're not far from Virginia City, but we're too far to try to carry Herbie."

Tennessee's eyes brightened. "I have it!" he said. "I'll put the spare tire on Herbie, and we'll go in on three wheels with me hanging out of the door."

"Can we do it?" Carole asked hopefully.

Jim jumped to his feet. "We can try!"

Late that night, Herbie "sailed" into Virginia City. No one was there to greet the car or its crew. The other drivers and the race officials had gone to sleep.

"You'd better catch a few hours sleep," Jim said. "Tennessee and I will see if we can get Herbie back into condition."

Carole smiled. "Thanks, but I'll stay with you two."

Jim took Carole's hand and said, "I figured you would, but I want you to take care of yourself. If you start to feel weak, let me know."

They worked through the night, and at dawn, Mr. Wu came to their work area. "Is everything all right?" he asked.

Softly, Jim said, "Mr. Wu, this little car gave us everything it's got. We patched it together now, but I don't know what to do. The poor little thing really has nothing left to give. It's your car, so what do you say?"

"When a wise man comes to last page," Mr. Wu said, "he closes the book."

Then Mr. Wu bowed and walked off, while Carole, Tennessee and Jim gratefully stared after him.

After a while, Carole turned to Jim and said, "You let that little car get under your skin, didn't you?"

"You know," Jim said slowly, "there is something real about that little car — something way out that doesn't even have a name. Still I don't understand why the little car picked a swollen-headed, second-rate driver like me."

"You stood up for it once," Carole said, moving close to Jim and then sliding into his arms. "Maybe it thought you were worth belonging to. I understand that."

Jim took her chin and tilted her face toward him. Then he kissed her.

"Well, isn't this nice," Thorndyke said, causing Jim and Carole to pull apart. "I really didn't mean to disturb you. I'll just take the little car and go."

"Take the little car?" Jim said. "What are you talking about?"

"I heard that you're out of the race," Thorndyke said. "So that makes me the new owner of the little car. I'll just drive it to my mechanics now, and you two can continue."

Jim clenched his fists and said, "Who made you the new owner of the car?"

Thorndyke glanced at Mr. Wu who just had returned to the work area. "Perhaps Mr. Wu cares to tell you how he wagered the little car on the outcome of the race."

Jim turned to Mr. Wu who said sadly, "I believed in the little car, too. I thought it would win. Even more honestly — I could not resist the odds."

Thorndyke stepped over to Herbie's side, smiling triumphantly. "Mr. Douglas," he said, "I suppose you would call this little beast a compact car. Well, you've never seen

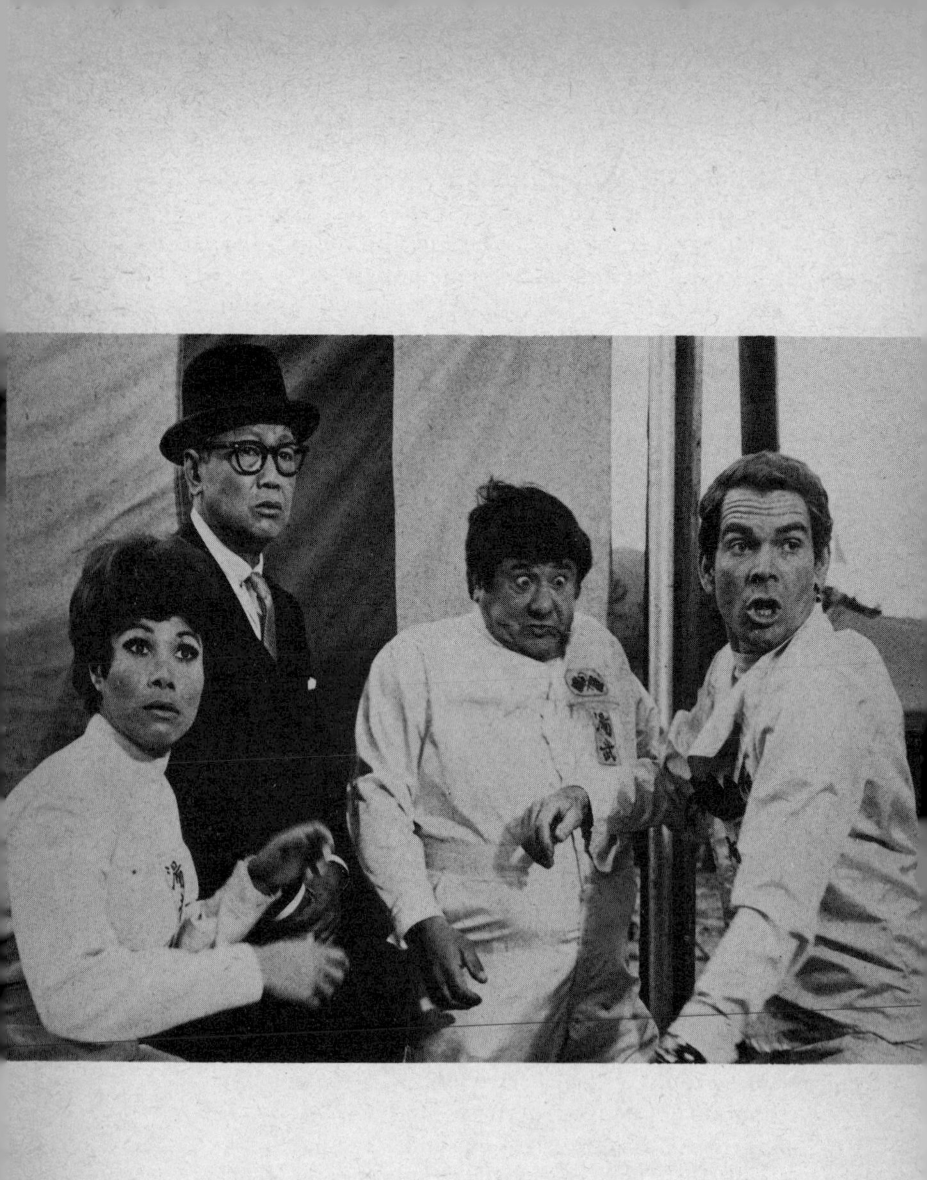

a compact car till you see what I'm going to do with this one! A friend of mine in San Francisco is going to work on your little car. I haven't decided yet whether I want it turned into an ash tray or a door mat, but I suppose I'd rather wipe my feet on it every day."

The thought seemed to excite Thorndyke, and he kicked hard at Herbie's door. Suddenly, Herbie started with a huge roar! The motor sounded as if it were new! Then the little car started after Thorndyke!

While this was happening, Carole, Mr. Wu, Tennessee, and Jim had watched in amazement, but Jim suddenly realized that even Thorndyke deserved to be saved. "Come on!" he told Wu.

The two men raced after Herbie and finally brought it to a halt by hanging onto its rear bumper.

"Small car very angry," Mr. Wu told Jim.

"And very strong," Jim added.

Mr. Wu smiled. "The second part of the race begins in thirty minutes," he said. "I think now we have chance to remove Egg Foo Yong off our faces!"

XII

WHEN THORNDYKE roared out of Virginia City on the second and final day of the race, Jim, Carole, and Tennessee were waiting at the starting line for a signal to begin, and Herbie's rear wheels were kicking up dust like a bull getting ready for a charge.

"Calm down, Herbie," Tennessee said. "Thorndyke came into town before us, so he has a right to leave before us. When that man with the flag signals to us, it'll be time to go — go like you've never gone before, little fellow!"

Herbie needed little coaxing. From that very first day that Jim had seen the little car, it hadn't liked Thorndyke, because of Thorndyke's meanness. So when the starter for Herbie dropped his flag, the little car shot out of Virginia City so fast that the race's judges had to check to see if a car had just flown past them.

As they started to pass cars, Tennessee noticed that Jim had more control over Herbie than he had had in all the other races. He also noticed that Jim was driving better than he had driven in several years.

"You're doing great," Carole told Jim, as they passed another car.

Jim shook his head back and forth. "No," he said. "No nice words until we pass Thorndyke, and if Herbie is going as fast as that needle says, we should catch up with Thorndyke at Whisky City."

Whisky City had been abandoned for almost half a century. It was a ghost town, and when Thorndyke wheeled into it, he found the old town's narrow streets difficult and dangerous. He wondered if the little car was nearby, and then he smiled to himself and shook his head, happy that he hadn't shared the silly thought with Havershaw.

At the same time, Jim was whipping Herbie through the back lots and narrowest lots in Whisky City.

"I think I just caught a glimpse of Thorndyke's car!" Jim said proudly.

"Where?" Carole said, stiffening slightly in her seat.

"You'll see in a minute," Jim said. Then he turned Herbie and drove through the back doors of what once had been a saloon.

Three seconds later, Herbie rammed through the saloon's front door and onto the road leading out of town.

"Don't look now," Carole warned, "but we are back in the lead in this race."

"Hurray for us!" Tennessee said. "I knew you could do it, Jim, and you, too, Herbie."

At the same time, Thorndyke told Havershaw, "Now we're behind again. I'm finished being Mr. Nice Guy."

"That's a good idea," Havershaw replied.

Thorndyke smiled, starting to slide the Apollo into position to pass Herbie. "As soon as Douglas hits that upgrade, we're going through."

53
53

"Let's go!" Carole said. "Thorndyke's moving up on us."

Jim looked at the gas pedal. It was down to the floor. "These mountain roads are tiring Herbie," he said. "I think we'll have to let him go by and then try to catch him on the way down."

Seconds later, Thorndyke whizzed past the little car and soon disappeared around one of the road's many curves.

"There's a logging area coming up soon," Thorndyke said. "If we have a worth-while lead, I'm going to stop. If I do, get out as fast as you can, Havershaw. We're going to stop Douglas, Miss Bennett, and Douglas' fat, dumb little friend once and for all!"

"How?"

"Leave that to me!"

Thorndyke skidded to a stop five minutes later, next to some logs on the side of the road. "Come on," he said. "We don't have much time."

The two men quickly picked a log and started rolling it onto the road. It was a huge log, and sweat poured from their bodies as they struggled to get it onto the road before the little car reached that spot.

"Are you sure this is wise, sir?" Havershaw asked.

"Shut up!" Thorndyke grunted. "Just push!"

Herbie suddenly shot around a curve, just as Thorndyke and Havershaw got the log in place. Then Havershaw dived off to safety at the side of the road. Thorndyke, though, wasn't so lucky. The little car's front bumper slammed into the log, and its luggage compartment lid flew open. The log hit Thorndyke's shins and its impact threw him forward into the open luggage compartment. Then the lid slammed shut on him.

Jim speedily shifted Herbie into reverse and backed away

53

from the log. Then he shifted back into a forward gear and went around the log and down the road, picking up speed as he went.

"Wasn't that Thorndyke?" Jim said, turning for a split second and glancing through Herbie's back window.

"I think so," Carole replied.

Jim frowned. "Where'd he go?"

"I don't know," Carole said. "It was like he disappeared.

Then the three of them heard a strange knocking sound coming from the front of the car.

"It sounds like one of the cylinders," Tennessee said.

"How could that be?" Jim asked. "The cylinders are in the back."

Tennessee nodded. "That is the point I find puzzling."

The knocking grew louder, and Carole put her ear to Herbie's dash. Then she snapped open the door of the glove compartment. Thorndyke's face, filled with rage, stared up at her. Surprised, she quickly shut the compartment door.

"Either we've got a TV in that compartment," she said, "or you've picked up the strangest luggage ever seen!"

Jim pulled to the side of the road and stopped. Then he and Tennessee climbed out and went to the front compartment. Thorndyke was inside, pushed together like a ball, so they lifted him out and rolled him over to a tree. As they pulled away, Tennessee saw Havershaw in the Apollo, skidding to a stop by the tree.

"Are you all right?" Havershaw asked, while he unrolled Thorndyke.

"You fool!" Thorndyke screamed. "If I lose this race, I lose my business to Wu! Where have you been?"

"I was in the car," Havershaw answered. "Where have you been?"

At the marker for the final quarter-mile, the Apollo pulled alongside Herbie. The beetle was weary. Jim had its gas pedal to the floor, but Herbie wasn't responding. Then the Apollo moved ahead slightly.

"Jim," Carole screamed, "he has the lead!"

"I know," Jim said sadly. "Herbie's tired."

Then Thorndyke glanced back at the little car and laughed.

"Did you see that, Herbie?" Tennessee whispered. "Thorndyke's laughing at you. He's laughing at all of us."

Herbie came to life! Its engine roared! With less than fifty yards to go, it pulled alongside Thorndyke's Apollo. Then Herbie's horn sounded! Thorndyke turned and saw the little beetle inch its way ahead of him. He stomped on his gas pedal! But it was too late! Herbie's front bumper had crossed the finish line!

When Jim stopped, Carole kissed and hugged him, while flashbulbs popped all around.

A few weeks later, Thorndyke's Imported European Motors had a new owner, and the new owner had two new mechanics.

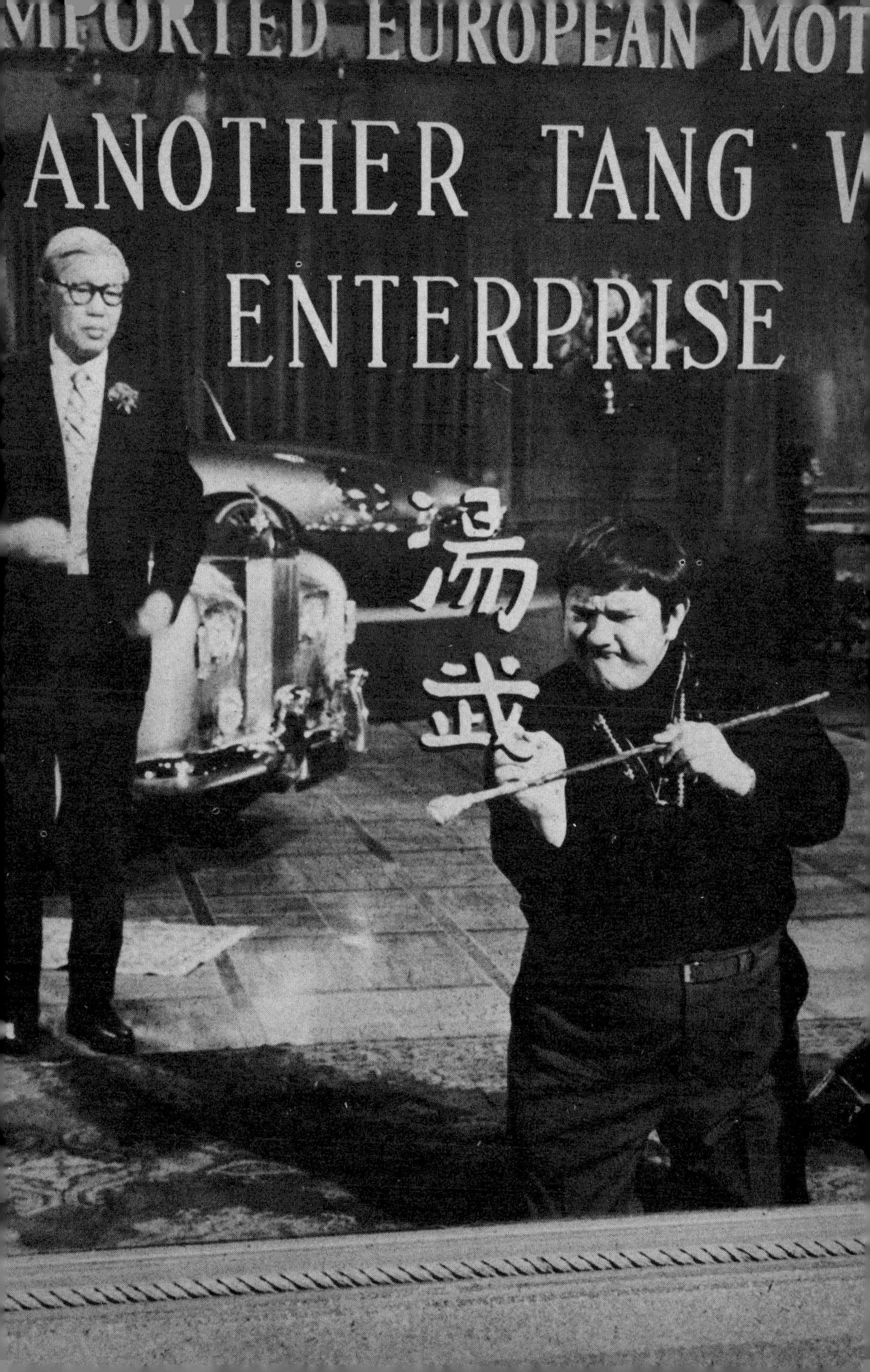

EUROPEAN
ANOTHER TANG
ENTERPRISE
湯武

Unfortunately, the mechanics, gentlemen named Thorndyke and Havershaw, didn't seem to work well together. They wasted a lot of time arguing about a race they had been in.

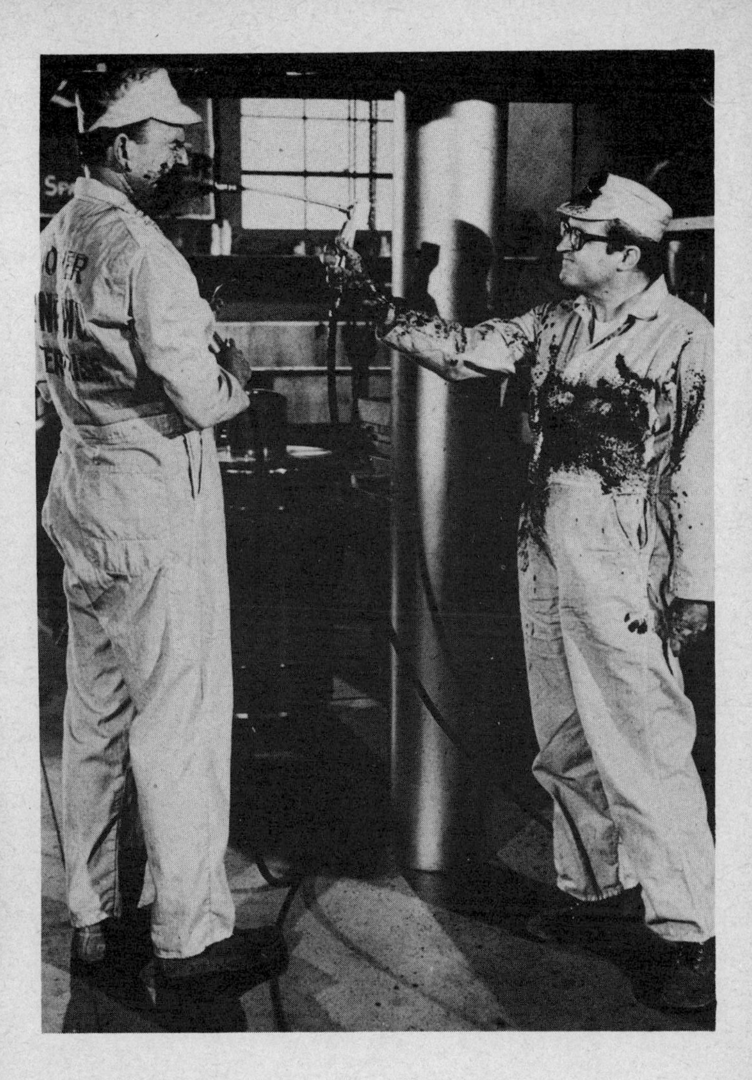

That same day, Carole and Jim got married and left for a honeymoon—at — Well, they let Herbie make that decision.

OFP 857

53